FOOTPRINTS IN

CW01512486

This is my sixth book . the previous themes, sc novels which were gene corporate environment.

But in this book, each of the four stories deals with a happening that might be described as supernatural, or ghostly.

So do ghosts really exist? If so can you talk to them? Can they talk to you? Of course I don't know the definitive answer, and I doubt whether anyone else does, but I definitely wouldn't say that they *don't* exist as twice in my lifetime I have experienced strange feelings or events that I would judge to have been unnatural. But were they ghostly? I have no idea but to my mind they certainly defied a normal explanation and so therefore I would be prepared to believe that they *may* have been and thus on that basis then yes, perhaps ghosts *do* exist.

The first three stories in this book are purely based upon my imagination. But within the fourth - The College - there is an element of one of the two strange happenings which I have experienced and to which I have referred above. Many years ago in the early days of my business career I, like the character in my story, did attend a Business Management College and there was undoubtedly a feeling of something peculiar on the top floor of the old house. Furthermore in one of the downstairs syndicate rooms unquestionably there was definitely a strange presence.

What it was I have no idea but there was a person or a manifestation to be seen in the room that wasn't really there and yet was there and could be seen. I know because I saw him.

I've never tried to explain or rationalise it and I just accept it for whatever it was - or wasn't! Now though it forms part of the fourth story although the rest of that tale is wholly imaginary.

So read and hopefully enjoy the four stories and then make up your own mind about ghosts and whether they exist or not?

The past is a ghost, the future a dream and all we have is now.
Bill Crosby.

For spirits freed from mortal laws will each Assume what sexes and shapes they please'
Alexander Pope.

Footprints in the Snow

A Book of Ghost Stories

Mike Upton

authorHOUSE®

AuthorHouse™ UK Ltd.
500 Avebury Boulevard
Central Milton Keynes, MK9 2BE
www.authorhouse.co.uk
Phone: 08001974150

This book is a work of fiction, People, places and situations are the figment of the author's imagination. Any resemblance to actual persons, living or dead or historical events is purely coincidental.

First published by AuthorHouse 8/11/2010

ISBN: 978-1-4520-5057-7 (sc)

This book is printed on acid-free paper.

Footprints in the Snow is dedicated to many people:-

- ➢ To my wife Brenda.

- ➢ To my daughters Catherine, Victoria and my grand-daughter Holly.

- ➢ To Sarah who was my pa and secretary and even though now we no longer work together is still always at the end of a phone or e-mail and more than willing to help me when I ask for her assistance, whether that be to solve computer issues, creating styles or logos, or just making me see the funny side of life.

- ➢ To the great team at AuthorHouse both in the UK and USA who as always offer such friendly efficient helpful support.

- ➢ Lastly to relatives, friends, acquaintances and others who continue to encourage me to write and publish more novels.

To all of the above may I say thank you very much.

======================

But finally and most importantly to
all my readers I hope you enjoy
Footprints in the Snow.

======================

MIKE UPTON

Contents

No object is mysterious. The mystery is in your eye.
Elizabeth Bowen.

FOOTPRINTS IN THE SNOW

CHAPTER 1

It sounded as though the wind had dropped from the fierce tempest of last night down to a much more gentle breeze. I slithered out of bed being careful to try and avoid waking Becky who was still fast asleep. The light was peeping through the curtains and as I padded over to the window to peer out I glanced at my watch which showed 7.25.

Easing the curtains a little apart I looked out. The snow was still falling but slowly and now only a few fluffy flakes were gently drifting down to settle on the thick carpet of white that was blanketing everything. As I looked around I estimated from the depth of snow that was sitting on the patio table below our bedroom that there must have been close on nine or ten inches. Everywhere I looked was beautiful. The sky was still grey and threatening but the whole winter scene was delightfully picturesque and just like a Christmas card picture.

I stayed there for several minutes. I could see some rabbit tracks on the lawn and there were a couple of blackbirds hopping about looking for food. Some blue and great tits were swinging around on the fat balls that we'd hung up and further down the garden I could see a pair of grey squirrels chasing each other on the ground before leaping onto a tree and disappearing into the upper reaches of the branches.

It was lovely just standing looking and as the radiator was beneath the window and I was standing close to it then I wasn't cold but after several minutes I turned to look at my wife who was still sleeping.

Walking slowly out of the room I went downstairs to make some tea for us both. As I waited for the kettle to boil I ruffled the head of our lovely golden retriever, opened the kitchen door to let her out, and I watched through the window as she scampered about running with her nose in the snow and then she spotted one of the squirrels which had come back to the ground and with a huge bark she shot up the garden and chased it up its tree again. I opened the door, whistled for her and as she was incredibly obedient she immediately stopped what she was doing and loped back to me coming indoors with a broad grin from ear to ear as she flopped down into her basket where she started to lick the snow off her paws. The kettle had now boiled so I also put a glass of fresh orange juice and some dry cheese crackers on the tray for Becky when I took it upstairs.

Carefully placing her mug of tea and the juice and crackers on her bedside table I was soon wriggling back into bed again where I sat up leaning against the headboard sipping the hot drink.

When I judged that her tea would have cooled from boiling hot to drinkable I leaned down, kissed her ear and whispered 'Morning darling'.

She stirred, opened her eyes, rolled over towards me and smiled.

'Morning Mr Rushworth'.

I kissed her lips gently and she smiled again.

'Tea, juice and biscuits await you my lady'.

'Thanks but I just need to pop to the loo first' and with a struggle and a wince she managed to sit up, swing her legs out of bed and make her way to our en-suite. She wasn't long and soon she waddled back and got into bed again.

'God I feel more like a whale everyday'.

'Being eight months pregnant with twins is bound to puff you up a bit'.

'Puff me up. Hells bells just look at me Jeff. I'm like a ....'

I silenced her protestations with another tender kiss and then as we drew apart I pulled down the duvet cover, leaned over and kissed her nightie covered bulging belly. 'You are utterly beautiful' I said softly.

'Liar' she laughed. 'I'm fat, I walk like a waddling duck, I've got swollen ankles, I keep needing to go and pee and ....'

Once again I stopped her statement about how she saw herself with another kiss and pulled her head onto my chest as I stroked her long auburn hair. 'Shhh I love you just the way you are. Now drink your tea'.

She looked up at me and muttered 'You are a nice man. I'm so glad I married you' and then with some significant effort she managed to turn onto her side and picking up the glass of juice drank that down in three or four large gulps following which she munched her way through the dry biscuits. Then picking up the mug of tea she wriggled back against me and sat there sipping it as I again stroked her hair.

It was nearly eight o'clock when she asked what I was planning to do today.

'Well after breakfast I must check some e-mails as I'm expecting the police and fire brigade reports on whether that chap started the fire in his shop deliberately as if he did then the insurers won't pay out'.

'Do you think he did?'

'Yes I do as he was up to his eyes in debt; his business had all but collapsed following the opening of that giant hardware superstore only a few hundred yards away and his wife had run off with another bloke and was suing him for divorce. I think he was at his wits end as he didn't have any money to pay her off and I reckon he saw this as a quick easy way to get some cash'.

'Poor man. You sound pretty sure though he did it'.

'Umm in all my years as an insurance investigator I think this is one of the most open and shut cases of attempted fraud that I've seen for a long time. Still we'll see.

Any rate after that I need to chop some more logs. I should have done it yesterday as you suggested but there we are I didn't so that's my next chore. Then I'll have a wander around and make sure the snow hasn't done any damage and I wouldn't be surprised if by then it wasn't close to lunch time. I think this afternoon I'll take Penny for a walk in the woods. Do you feel up to coming?'

'No darling I don't but yes you go. It'll be lovely wandering through the woods after the snow. I'll stay here and be lazy and look after our soon to arrive son and daughter. Actually I really ought to get that latest article finished otherwise Henry will start creating and chasing and complaining'.

Henry was one of her editors. Becky was a freelance writer who worked from home submitting a variety of "women orientated" articles to various newspapers and magazines as well as writing a couple of regular weekly columns, one for a Sunday red top and the other for one of the daily broadsheets. She was a good journalist and enjoyed her work but I knew that the impending birth was making her find the energy to work more difficult.

'Sounds good to me' I said encouragingly. 'Now my girl I think I'll present myself to the day' and with a grin and giving her another little kiss I rolled out of bed and threw the curtains wide open.

Becky sat up and peered out. One of the advantages of living in this little old cottage which we'd bought a few months ago was that the windows both upstairs and down were set extremely low and so from our bed it was quite possible to see out onto our large garden which backed onto open fields. In the distance about a mile away could be seen the woods which I'd spoken about earlier.

I showered, shaved and after I'd dressed Becky heaved herself out of bed and headed to the shower.

When I was downstairs I put a couple of rashers of bacon, an egg, some mushrooms and a tomato in the frying pan, two slices of bread in the toaster; popped a couple of croissants in the oven to warm for Becky, ground some coffee beans and turned on the coffee maker.

To my amazement all was ready at about the same time just as Becky wearing loose fitting top, maternity slacks and some flat heeled shoes lumbered into the kitchen then went over to kneel down and stroke Penny.

I poured the coffee and suggested that my wife joined me at the table which she did.

'Umm lovely. Thank you darling' she smiled as she picked up her coffee mug.

When we'd finished I cleared away and then we both walked to our little study which led off the sitting room. We have two desks side by side each with our laptops so as Becky brought up "Word" and started to get creative I fired up my e-mail. There were several new ones in the "inbox" and after deleting the junk and spam I flicked through the others until I found the one I wanted.

I skimmed through the report quickly and then printed it off. Once I had the paper copy I carefully read it thoroughly from cover to cover. Yep just as I thought, the Fire Brigade evidence was clear. The fire had been started deliberately. So there we are. No payout from the insurer and next week discussion with the police as to whether they would charge the man with arson.

I spent about half an hour on a few other reports and e-mails and then standing up I stretched, looked at Becky and said I was off to start log chopping.

'Ok be careful don't chop yourself will you love' she grinned.

I put on a thick sweater, a waterproof jacket, an extra pair of socks and pushed my feet into my wellies. Collecting a flat cap and my gloves I clicked my tongue at Penny who was looking expectantly at me. Immediately she jumped up and followed me to the door and was soon gambolling and bouncing around again in the snow. I bent down and made a snow ball which I threw to her. She saw it coming and caught it in the mouth but immediately spat it out with a look of some disgust.

Ignoring her antics I walked to the woodshed which was situated to the side of the cottage. The snow was too deep to get the door open so my first task was to go to the garage and collect a shovel and soon I'd cleared enough of the snow to open the woodshed door. But before starting on the logs I decided that I ought to clear some more snow, so half an hour later I'd cleared a path around the cottage, down the front path to the lane and two tracks where the car tyres would run from the garage to the lane so we could get the cars out.

Now it was time to return to the woodshed and so I spent the next hour or so happily whacking an axe into wood to create logs. Last Spring I'd had a huge quantity of rough sawn timber delivered which had to be chopped into smaller sizes to fit our woodburner.

Eventually I had a big pile of chopped logs, so carefully stacking most of them back in the woodshed at the front where I could easily get them when needed, I loaded the wheelbarrow with others, wheeled them to the front door and tipped them onto the large church type porch. I repeated this process several times and then spent some time neatly stacking the pile of logs there. Going indoors and being ticked off by Becky for not removing my wellies as she'd chosen just that moment to walk into the hallway, I sheepishly did as instructed then spent a few minutes minus rubber boots carrying some of the porch logs into the sitting room to stack beside the woodburner. So now I had my logs organised; a very large chopped pile in the woodshed; a reasonably large pile on the porch and a small quantity in the house ready for use.

Next I returned outside and walked around our large

garden shaking snow off some of the shrubs which were bent over from its weight. I studied the cottage from all angles and could see no problems with the snow and the roof so satisfied that all was well I called Penny and the two of us went inside where Becky had some homemade vegetable soup bubbling on the Aga. She also had some hot just baked rolls on the table and soon the two of us were sitting enjoying our lunch.

Afterwards we went into the sitting room and sat reading the Sunday papers.

'Oh look this has a piece I wrote' she said handing me the red top open at the women's section.

'What's it about?' I asked as I got up to walk over to her and take it.

'Sex between couples where the woman is in the latter stages of pregnancy. I wrote it at least a month ago and I'd forgotten all about it'.

'Are you pleased with the way it's come out?'

'Yes but, err it's perhaps a bit raunchy now I see it in the cold light of newsprint' she chuckled. 'Almost made me blush when I read it'.

'I think I'd better check it out then hadn't I?' and taking the proffered paper I plonked down and read what she'd written. She was right as she'd been somewhat explicit in her recommendations and suggestions as to what couples should do to satisfy themselves sexually in the latter stages of pregnancy.

We ourselves had stopped making love together somewhere between the sixth and seventh months as Becky was worried about the baby even though we found positions that meant I wasn't lying on top of her belly. Actually in the earlier months it had been fun experimenting with positions and techniques that enabled penetration and so satisfaction for me but minimised discomfort for her but there had come a point where one night after we'd finished and moved apart she'd asked if we could stop now until after the baby was born. Seeing my look of sudden and exaggerated disappointment she'd pulled me to her.

'Hey don't look so worried Jeff. I'll make it good and get your rocks off for you in other ways rather than making love properly' and she'd been as good as her word from then on.

Becky's journalistic career had been quite varied before she became a freelance as she was now, and in the past she'd been on the permanent staff of various newspapers and magazines including one six month stint with a sexually explicit 'lads mag' and since that time now she was freelance she often wrote quite frank and uninhibited articles about relationships and sex and this was one of those. As I put the paper down she looked at me.

'Well?'

'Umm'.

'What do you mean umm?'

I walked over and sat next to her on the settee. 'Umm means I think that for me to fully appreciate what you've been writing about then I think some practical demonstration and explanation is required'.

'Oh do you' she laughed leaning forward and resting her forehead against mine.

'Yes I do. Now what was it you said about the pregnant woman not being afraid to initiate seduction during the day instead of waiting for bed time?'

'Did I say that?' she asked with her eyes wide.

'Uh huh. So do you know I think I might like to be seduced during the day? In fact I think right now might be a very good time ...... wouldn't you say?'

'Oh I don't know about that' she frowned but with a twinkle in her eye.

'Important to practice what you preach you know'.

'You think so do you?' she grinned.

'Yes absolutely. After all if thousands of couples this very day are doing some or all of the things you've written about then you really ought to find out if it works properly. I mean writing about it is one thing, but actually doing it is quite another. Can you imagine? At this very moment all over the country there will be men and women tangled together with the paper in one hand and trying to do what you suggest' I laughed.

'Bless. Right come here then' and as I looked at her she kissed me, initially softly and tenderly but soon she pressed her lips on mine much harder as her hands went to the back of my neck and started stroking and massaging before she clambered off the settee and knelt in front of me.

In a surprisingly short time she had undressed me until I was lying back just in my boxers as her kissing had moved from lips and face to chest, nipples and belly while one of her hands started rummaging around inside my pants quickly inducing an erection.

'I think we'd better just let him out to play don't you? Lift up' and as I raised my bum off the cushion she slid the boxers down to my knees. 'Aah now that's better' she said as her hand gently clasped around me.

She was gentle and erotic especially when her other

hand took my balls and massaged them as she lowered her head and let her lips engulf me.

Her mouth was soft, warm and tender and she worked on me with a care and gentle intensity that was wonderful but after a while I asked 'Is there something that you'd like me to do for you?' but without letting go of me she just shook her head and continued what she was doing.

After I'd finished, she smiled and asked quietly 'Now my darling was that alright for you?'

Becky had always enjoyed and been good at giving oral sex and her slow tender hand and oral loving of me today had been wonderful as she had fulfilled her promise made some weeks ago by using all of those skills on me this afternoon. So I leaned down and said it had been great and thank you, before leaning further forward to kiss her.

'But Becks are you sure you don't want me to do something like that for you?'

'No my happiness and pleasure is in giving you satisfaction and knowing that I am doing what I think is right for our babies. I can happily go a few weeks without sex or having orgasms and it isn't a problem to me but ....'

'But?'

'But just you wait my man until I've delivered these two' and she tapped her swollen tummy 'as when I'm all back to normal down below and my sexual needs have returned and I'm horny, hyped up and ready for it, then my darling you are going to have to make love to me over and over again to make up for what I'm missing now'.

'I assure you it will be an enormous pleasure' I chuckled.

'Good. I am really very glad to hear it. Now unless you want me to do it again for you' and she took hold of my limp prick and raising her eyebrows put on a querying expression but hearing me mutter that I was fine she grinned and continued 'then I think it's time we put this away don't you?' and with a little giggle she eased my boxers up and covered me. Patting my genitals over the pants she struggled to her feet and leaning down pulled my face to hers and we kissed.

'Are you alright?' I wanted to know. 'After all kneeling can't have been too comfortable for you in your condition?'

'No actually it's fine. Kneeling is good and don't forget that many women give birth like that especially if they are using a birthing pool?'

'Oh ok that's all right then'.

'Now I think you should go for your walk and leave me to have a little rest. After all it's quite tiring satisfying my husband's sexual needs!'

'Fine' I replied as she slowly, carefully and obviously uncomfortably lowered herself back onto the settee and watched as I dressed again.

'Thanks' I said quietly as now re-dressed I leaned down and dropped a quick kiss on her forehead.

'All part of the wifely service my lord and master. Now go on, off you go. Time to take the dog for a walk'.

It was only a matter of minutes to dress for the outdoors, collect Penny and set off. It had stopped snowing and the dark grey clouds had gone. The sky was clear blue and although cold it was great to be out with the dog who frolicked and romped along happily, sometimes running far ahead of me then coming back and rounding me up, before charging off to one side of me or the other.

She was happy and so was I as we strode out for the distant woods.

CHAPTER 2

It really was quite wonderful being out in the snow and sunshine. Everything was bright, sparkling and beautiful with wondrous shapes created by the snow especially where the wind had blown it into drifts. Penny ran, jumped and bounded about playing and exploring and clearly having a fantastic time.

After about fifteen minutes I reached the edge of the woods. There were several in this part of West Norfolk and I selected a track leading into the darker inside of the one we were going to walk through today. Here the snow in many places was less deep as the trees or dense shrubbery had formed barriers and as I got further into the wood although the clearings were deep with snow most of the rest varied from deep to quite light coverings. Penny and I strode along following the track which was pristine and had no marks or prints on it except for an occasional rabbit's paw prints and in one place there were clear markings of a fox having chased a rabbit.

Several times I stopped to take pictures of the snow scenes on my fancy new mobile camera phone.

I'd never known how big in acreage the wood was although it was pretty large but I felt quite safe and unlikely to get lost as I followed the track. After all this track went right through the wood and it wasn't the first time that I'd walked here with the dog. So on we went and as we headed up a slight incline Penny who had been charging about to my right suddenly gave a bark and ran over to walk beside me.

Together we continued up the rise as she started growling and raised her hackles. She remained close to me and no longer ran around but started to walk more slowly and seemed to be almost deliberate in the way that she was carefully placing her paws on the ground.

Suddenly as we neared the top of the incline I could see over the summit and there coming towards us was a person with a dog beside them. If anything Penny seemed more concerned which was surprising as she was very well trained, didn't bother with other dogs and when given the command "leave" would just rub noses and walk past without fuss or difficulty. But now her low growls became more intense, her hackles remained fully raised and she stopped completely still and alternated her looks from me to the distant figure that was coming towards us along the track.

'Hey come on' I commanded as I looked down and back at her while still walking forward but she remained where she was. Turning back to her I stroked her ear and tried to encourage her to come forward with me but she remained adamantly still, so taking the slip lead out of my pocket which I always carry in case of emergency or need, I put it around her neck and tugged her forward with a crisp 'Come on'. Her disinclination to do so was obvious so I gave the lead a sharp tug and reluctantly she moved but still hanging back and quietly growling at the back of her throat.

As I walked on down the other side of the incline the person was now quite close and I could see that it was a girl of probably twelve or thirteen with a black and white collie dog on a lead by her side.

She looked straight ahead as she walked and as she got closer I thought that her clothing was rather old fashioned because she had a dark blue gabardine raincoat, the sort that schoolgirls used to wear to school years ago. On her head was a grey beret with a little badge at the front and her feet were in black wellies, again looking rather old fashioned compared to the sort of brightly coloured wellies or fashion boots which teenage girls generally wore these days. I noticed that her face was very pale. White with no colour at all, and she didn't turn to look at me or seem to even acknowledge that I was there. Penny by now was almost frantic trying to tug herself free from the slip lead and twisting herself to stand behind me. Surely she wasn't frightened of the girl's dog?

As we got closer I smiled and said 'Hello'. Continuing towards me the girl said nothing so I spoke again. 'Isn't it glorious to be out with a dog in these woods with the sun shining and the deep snow?'

She slowed her walk and spoke quietly but didn't look at me. 'Not for me'.

'Oh why's that?'

'Because they won't find me'.

'Who won't find you?'

'All those that are looking'.

'Are you lost then? Do you need some help? Would you like me to walk you somewhere?'

'No thank you'.

'Wait' and I took my camera phone out of my pocket and aimed it at her. 'Look at me'. Slowly she turned her head. I clicked. 'Thank you. Now are you *quite* sure you're alright?'

She nodded then turned to face the front again and started to walk away from me with her collie still by her side. I watched her go pondering on what a strange exchange of conversation it had been. In a way I was slightly concerned that she might have been lost but I didn't see how she could be as the track was wide, clear and easy to walk on and led through the woods from one side to the other. Nevertheless I remained uneasy and also thought it strange that her dog hadn't once seemed to even look at Penny or me but remained looking ahead in the direction that they were heading, as indeed had the girl except for that brief moment when she turned towards me for the photograph.

As they went away Penny started to relax. Her hackles flattened again she stopped growling and resumed a normal stance. The girl disappeared from my sight as she walked down the side of the incline up which I'd come. Something still bothered me though and so I turned round and trotted back up the incline but at the top as I looked for her there was no sign of her at all.

Trying to remember if there had been a side track or path which she might have taken I thought that there must have been so I guessed that was why I couldn't see her now. Shrugging I turned round to continue my walk but as I set off I suddenly noticed something very odd.

Stretching ahead of me was the track along which the girl and her dog had come towards me but there were no marks in the snow. No footprints. No footsteps. No paw prints. Nothing. The snow was white, virgin, untouched and utterly unmarked.

Frowning I turned and ran back to the top of the incline and looked back the way I'd come. There clearly showing in the snow were mine and Penny's prints, but where the girl and her dog had walked past us and then away there was nothing. It was as if they had never existed, nor walked past me.

I shivered involuntarily then speaking more loudly than really needed commanded 'Come on Pen girl on we go' and she leapt ahead relaxed, excited and now completely back to normal. But all along the track as we walked there were no foot or paw prints from the girl and her dog. None at all. The snow was unmarked.

Eventually we came out of the woods, as the track which I had taken apart from a few twists and turns basically just went straight through from one side to the other. We turned right and walked across the edge of a field to a small road which we marched along for a mile or so until we came to a crossroads where we turned right once more and about forty minutes later our village came into view and shortly I was stamping on the rear porch to get the snow off my boots, grabbing an old towel that hung there to dry the dog and soon I was indoors stripping off my waterproofs, sweaters and thick socks in the kitchen before settling Penny into her basket and tip-toeing into the sitting room where Becky was asleep on the settee.

As I didn't want to wake her I quietly lowered myself into an armchair and looked across at her. It never ceased to amaze and delight me that she had said yes when I asked her to marry me as she was stunningly lovely, lively, fun, had the pick of men but had fallen in love with me and we were very happily married. Now she still looked beautiful even though she was bulging enormously in the belly area and I enjoyed looking over to her as I went through in my mind the rather odd encounter on the track in the woods.

It was about half an hour later when Becky awoke,

stretched, grumbled as she held her tummy and wriggled herself into an upright position.

'Hi would you like some tea or coffee or a soft drink?'

'A cup of tea would be marvellous. Good walk?'

'Yes but something odd happened. I'll tell you in a minute when I've made your tea'.

'Lovely thanks' she smiled shortly after that as I handed her a steaming mug of tea, then she winced as she fidgeted to get into a comfortable position.

'So what was this odd thing that happened then?'

'Look I know this is going to sound very strange but I met this girl'.

'Oh so you've started to have secret assignations with some sexy blonde to have a quick passionate roll in the snow have you? And there was me thinking that I'd completely satisfied your carnal needs before you went out' she chuckled.

'Yes you did' I laughed. 'No meeting this girl was really odd'.

I then spent the next few minutes explaining what I'd seen and especially about there being no footprints from the girl or the dog. Becky suggested that maybe a breeze had blown snow to fill in the footmarks as soon as they'd been made but I assured her that there had been no wind or breeze and that even if there had been then it wouldn't have completely obliterated every single footprint or paw print. We chatted about it for a few more minutes until she brought the subject to a close by saying 'Well I don't know Jeff. One of life's mysteries I guess. Now I'm going to have a bath. Shall I leave the water in for you?'

Putting the unknown girl out of my mind I read

the paper for a while then wandered upstairs and into the bathroom where Becky was lying back enjoying her bath.

'Wash your back and a neck massage madam?'

'Ooh yes both please' and she sat up and leaned forward. Sitting on the side of the bath I soaped a flannel and then gently washed her back and neck before washing off the suds and replacing flannel and soap with my hands I kneaded her neck, shoulders and upper back. She'd always loved being massaged like this in the bath or in bed or just when she was sitting in a chair and I stood behind her. Indeed many times in the past my massaging of her had led to some delightful lovemaking sessions but today in view of her condition and the fact that she'd so adequately satisfied me earlier I just concentrated on giving her a good relaxing time.

When I finished I helped her stand up and getting a nice warm towel I wrapped her in it, kissed her wet face then as she turned to walk out of the bathroom I gave her a little pat on her towel covered bottom. She smiled, blew me a kiss and left the room so I stripped off and was soon lying back in the still warm water where I reflected initially on my happy life, my love for Becky, the forthcoming birth of our first children but also inevitably for a moment on the girl in the woods.

'Hey are you going to spend all night in there you sexy thing?' asked Becky a quarter of an hour later now dressed in maternity jeans and a tee shirt as she stuck her head round the door and looked me up and down.

'No just a few more minutes till I get out. I'm enjoying lying here relaxing, soaking and thinking about you and our future children'.

She walked in and perched on the side of the bath.

'Hey careful you don't slip' I warned.

'No I'm fine. I just like to look at you when you're naked. You know Jeff you've got a lovely body' and she leant forward and ran a finger down my forehead, nose, lips, chin, neck, chest, belly and into my pubic hair but teasingly she didn't go any lower and I watched her pink fingernail as it slowly traced its way back up my body pausing to touch my belly button and then move to circle each of my nipples before she took it to her own lips, planted a kiss on it and transferred that to my lips. 'I am so lucky being your wife. I do love you'.

'Mmm me too' I said softly.

'Shall I leave you for a while to enjoy your relaxing soak then?'

'No stay and talk to me' and so we did for a few minutes. 'Right' I said as we came to a pause in the conversation 'stand aside wench. Your lord and master is about to arise' and seeing her quizzically raise one eyebrow I grinned and added 'from the bath. You young lady have a dirty mind at times!'

'So?' she giggled.

'So' I said standing up.

With a theatrical gesture she gave a little squeal and covered her eyes while she groped for a towel off the hot rail to hand to me. 'Cover yourself sir as it surely isn't good for a lady in my delicate condition to see a man without any clothes upon himself. It might bring uncontrollable lustful thoughts to me' she simpered.

Taking the towel I wrapped it around my waist and told her that I was covered and peeking through a little gap in her fingers she nodded and taking my hand waited until I'd pulled out the bath plug then led me into our bedroom where she sat on the bed and smiled at me.

I unwrapped the towel and used it to dry my hair and as I did so she said 'I just love to see your willy when it's all floppy wobbling around while you do that. It sort of establishes a life and movement all of its own rather than just hanging around down there'.

'Glad to be able to offer you such entertainment madam' I smirked then turning away I picked up my comb and soon had sorted my hair into some semblance of order. 'Hey do you fancy going to the pub for a little while this evening or might you not be feeling up to it?'

'Yes fine there's nothing on tv tonight and I'm feeling ok. Fat and lumbering but ok so yes let's wander down there for a drink before supper but I hope you're going to put on some clothes?'

'You don't think the people in the pub would like to see me like this then eh?'

'They might but I think you'd run the risk of getting a frost bitten willy and that wouldn't be any good for either of us would it?'

'Ok clothes it is then' I replied pulling on a clean pair of pants.

So just after seven we set off for the half mile walk to the other end of the village and the Kings Head where we were soon enveloped in the warm slightly fuggy beery atmosphere that exists in pubs which have a blazing log fire at one end, several customers, a slightly damp floor from lots of wet or snowy feet and a number of people drinking pints or sipping glasses of wine.

'Hello there' Mary the landlady greeted us cheerfully. 'It's nice to see the two of you again. Keeping well are you

Becky love? I must say you look positively blooming and it's not long now is it till you pop 'em out? Right so what can I get you both?'

I settled for a pint of one of their guest beers and Becky had a pineapple juice and soda water. We found a table in the corner near the fire and sat drinking and chatting together. My beer seemed to go down rather quickly so although Becky didn't want another drink I went to the bar and ordered a half. While Mary was pouring it she asked what we'd been doing during the day and so I found myself telling her about the strange girl in the woods.

'That does sound odd doesn't it?' she queried with a puzzled expression. 'I'll ask around and see if anyone knows anything about a phenomenon like that. Ted and I have only been here for three years so I am still learning about local history and stories. If I hear anything I'll let you know. Now anything else?'

I said no, paid and was soon sitting with Becky again and just after eight we left and wandered slowly hand in hand back through the village.

Our cottage looked lovely and welcoming in the night as there was a bright moon, the windows were illuminated throwing a warm yellow glow to the outside and when we opened the door and walked in everything was warm and cosy.

Once indoors again we got supper together and we'd just finished eating our chicken risotto when there was a knock at the door.

Looking puzzled I got up from the table and walked into our little hallway and opened the door. Outside there stood a worried looking middle aged man and woman.

'Err hello we're sorry to trouble you at this time of night and on a Sunday as well, but I believe you saw a girl in the woods today?' said the man.

'Yes I did'.

'Do you think we could come in for a moment? It is really important. Please?'

There was such an expression of anxiousness on both of their faces that I immediately said yes and stood aside to allow them into the hall.

'Come through we'd just finished eating' I said as I led the way into the main room which had our dining table at one end and the rest was sitting room. Becky stood up with a baffled expression.

'These two people want a word about what I saw in the woods this afternoon'.

'What the girl?'

'Uh huh'.

'Hello' said the unknown woman. 'I am sorry to interrupt you but we would be ever so grateful for a few minutes of this gentleman's time' and she looked at me.

'Right well look I'm Jeff and this is Becky. Now how can I help you?'

'I'm Roy and this is my wife Margaret' said the man pointing to himself and the woman. 'Could you tell us what you saw? You see after you left the pub this evening Mary the landlady spoke to old Fred who's lived in this village all his life and knows everything. She told him what you said you'd seen and Fred come round straight away to tell us. So would you just tell us what you saw in the woods?'

I was about to ask why they wanted to know when Becky spoke.

'Look sit down. Would you like some coffee as we were about to have a cup?'

'No thank you. It's very kind of you but we just would like to know what, err Jeff wasn't it?' and when Margaret saw me nod continued 'what he saw'.

As they sat down Becky took our empty dinner plates into the kitchen and I heard her fill the kettle as I sat opposite the two strangers and started to speak.

'I was with Penny our dog. We went into the woods and were walking on a track that goes right through from one side to the other. Somewhere around the middle there is a little rise and when I got to the top I saw a person walking towards me. As they got close I could see it was a girl. I guess she was about twelve, thirteen maybe and she was wearing school uniform. But it was somewhat old fashioned not the type of thing school kids of that age wear nowadays'.

'Can you describe what she was wearing?'

'Yes a blue gabardine mac with a grey beret. Oh and black wellies. She had a dog with her, a collie'.

'Oh my God' whispered the man opposite me his hands trembling and I saw that his wife had gone white.

'Look what's this all about? Why do you want to know this?'

'Sorry we should have explained. Our little girl disappeared several years ago with our dog. Although there was an extensive police search and all the neighbours helped, little Anna was never found'.

'Yes' continued the wife 'I was feeling unwell and so Anna offered to take Rex, our dog, out for a walk. We live on the other side of those woods in the next village.

She left about three o'clock and that was the last time that I or anyone ever saw her'.

'Good God' I muttered quite astounded at this revelation.

'She would be twenty six now as it was fourteen years ago she disappeared and she was twelve at the time. It was the sixteenth of January when she disappeared. The same as today's date. The sixteenth of January'.

I was dumbfounded. 'But I saw her. I spoke to her'.

'You *spoke* to Anna?' queried Roy with an utterly bemused look on his face.

'Yes'.

'What did you say? Did she speak to you?'

'Yes. I can't remember exactly what I said. I think I said hello and that it was a lovely day for a walk in the snow. Yes that's it. That's what I said. But she said it wasn't and when I asked why she replied something about no-one being able to find her'.

'No-one being able to find her? Did she say anything else?'

'I don't think so. But look I took a picture of her on my phone'.

'A photo? Can we see it?'

'Sure hang on' and getting up I walked over to the side table, picked up my phone, scanned through to "pictures" and soon had the image of the girl on the screen. 'Here you are look' and I held the phone out to Margaret.

She took it, stared at it for a moment then giving a little cry collapsed on the floor. Roy immediately knelt down by her muttering 'She's fainted', picked up the phone and looking at the screen said 'Holy God above it's Anna. Anna baby where are you?' and he'd also now gone white as a sheet.

'Would she like some water maybe?' queried Becky as Roy gently slapped his wife's face.

'Yes please' and at that moment Margaret's eyes flickered open and she tried to sit up.

'It's her isn't it?' she said looking at Roy who helped her firstly sit up, then get up and move to an armchair where she sat white as the snow outside staring at me, then at Roy and then at Becky who handed the distressed woman a glass of cold water.

Nodding her thanks she took some sips. 'You saw our daughter. No-one has seen her since she and Rex disappeared. How could it be that you saw her today?'

'I don't know' I replied now feeling somewhat uncomfortable and looking at Becky who came over and held my hand as she stood beside me.

'Was there anything else? Did you see anyone else? Can you remember any other things?'

'Well there was one odd thing' I said slightly hesitantly as Roy and Mary looked at me expectantly.

'Yes. Go on, please. What odd thing?'

'There were no footprints. In the snow I mean. Where the girl walked, well and the dog also. There were no footmarks. No footprints from her or paw prints from the dog'.

They queried what I meant so I repeated what I'd said and they just looked puzzled as they stared at each other.

'Thank you for seeing us tonight' Margaret said quietly after a moment or two. 'We'll be going now but I don't understand it at all'.

'No I simply can't believe that you saw our little Anna after all these years' added Roy shaking his head in disbelief. 'It's not possible'.

I didn't know what to say and just looked at each of the two sad parents in front of me.

'Thank you for seeing us tonight. Would you mind if I mentioned this to the police in the morning?' asked Roy. 'After all they've never closed the case file on her disappearance. Will you keep the picture on your phone for me? You know, not delete it or anything?'

'Yes I'll keep the picture. In fact if you hang on a minute I'll upload it to my computer and print you off a copy' and going to the desk in our little study area off the main living room, I plugged in the cable to connect the phone to the laptop and after a few clicks saw that the image was coming onto the screen. I switched on the printer, pressed "print" and moments later the picture was rolling slowly out of the machine. I took it and without checking it walked back into the sitting room.

'Here you are' holding it out to them.

'Thanks. You are so kind' Margaret spoke quietly as she held out her hand for the picture and looked at it. 'Her face isn't there?' she said.

'Sorry what do you mean?' I asked.

'Look there is nothing between her beret and her coat. Nothing it's blank. No face'.

Taking the picture back I looked at it and she was right. There was simply a void where the child's face had been. 'Sorry something must have gone wrong with the printer. I'll run off another' and moving back into the study I picked up the mobile, paged to the photograph and stared in amazement as it was now the same as the printed copy. The child's face had disappeared as had her legs. All that was there was the beret, the mac and the wellies. Between the three items, just voids. Indeed you could see trees and shrubs behind where the girl had stood through the spaces where her face and legs no longer showed. It was weird. Her face and legs had been there earlier on the phone and of course when I met her but now there was the incongruous scene of a beret apparently completely unsupported, a mac standing up by itself and hovering above a pair of wellies. There was also no sign of the dog.

Anna and Rex had simply disappeared again.

Going back into the sitting room I explained and showed Roy, Mary and Becky the phone and we were all equally puzzled.

'It must have messed up part of the picture somehow when you uploaded it' suggested Becky.

'Well I don't know what it's done but only part of the picture is there now'.

'We'll be going now then' said Mary quietly.

'Yes thank you again. I'll talk to the police in the morning if that's alright?' Roy commented quietly.

I said it was fine to talk to the police as I showed them out, then watched as they walked away down the lane, two sad people walking slowly holding onto each other not only to help themselves avoid slipping in the snow but also I imagine for comfort and support.

CHAPTER 3

It was mid morning on the following day and I was in a meeting with a client when my mobile rang. Checking the screen I didn't recognise the number.

'Hello?'

'Mr Rushworth?'

'Yes speaking'.

'Good morning sir. My name is Detective Inspector Lloyd. I am calling you about an event that apparently occurred yesterday in some woods close to your home where I understand you saw a little girl?'

'Yes that's right I did'.

'Little Anna's parent called me this morning and I have just finished a meeting with them. I don't know where you are at the moment sir but I think it is pretty important that we meet and quickly. I believe her father Roy explained that Anna went missing fourteen years ago and has never been seen since'.

'Yes he did. Well I'm in Colchester at the moment but I could postpone the rest of my appointments for the day and return to Norfolk if you wish'.

'I would be most grateful if you'd do that sir'.

We agreed a time to meet at our home and then I rang Becky and explained the call I'd just received and she said that the police had rung our home first and she'd given them my mobile number. Telling her that I was coming home I rang off, finished the meeting I was having and getting in my car set off for our home near Swaffham arriving around twelve thirty as agreed with the policeman.

Outside our cottage were two police cars, a police

Range Rover, a white Transit van and a smaller van with **POLICE DOG UNIT** on the side. Every vehicle seemed to be full of policemen or policewomen. Getting out of my car I walked towards the cottage as a tall well dressed man in his forties got out of one of the cars and approached me holding out his hand.

'Mr Rushworth?'

'Yes that's me' I agreed shaking the proffered hand.

'Hello sir. We spoke earlier. I'm Detective Inspector Martin Lloyd. Can we go inside for a few minutes and then you can tell me and a colleague what you told Anna's parents last night'.

He beckoned towards the cars and someone else got out and joined us introducing herself as Detective Sergeant Tara Boyson. We went indoors and I introduced the two police officers to Becky and then invited them to sit down.

'Right sir. First I have to ask you one most important question and I want you to think very carefully before you answer. Alright?' I nodded. 'Is this some sort of practical joke that you are playing because if it is then it isn't at all funny?'

'No it isn't. I simply told Margaret and Roy what I'd seen and then I showed them the photograph that I took when I met the girl'.

'But for you to claim that you've seen a child that's been missing for fourteen years simply isn't believable is it?'

'Well whether you believe it or not that is exactly what happened! I was walking through the woods with our dog Penny and I saw the child and her dog. Yesterday. In the woods'.

He looked hard at me for at least a minute then nodded. 'Ok sir. So now tell *us* precisely what you saw. Take your time and try and remember everything please'.

'I can do better than that. I'll show you what I saw' and taking my mobile phone out of my pocket I flicked through to the picture of Anna but the picture showed no child, no mac, no wellies, no beret. Nothing. Just the snow, the trees, the shrubs and part of the track.

'I don't understand' I said frowning and then I explained what was puzzling me about the picture. After that I told them about my walk yesterday, meeting the girl and her dog, speaking with the child and then her walking off. I added the point about no footprints in the snow from her or her dog and finally I also added the explanation of Penny's strange behaviour.

The two police didn't ridicule me. They questioned, they probed and then the Sergeant extracted something from her slim briefcase and handed it to me.

'Is this the print that you made yesterday evening from your phone and gave to Anna's parents, Roy and Margaret?'

'Yes there you are look. There are the child's clothes but when I met her I saw her face, and her hands and her legs. She was complete and whole. The only odd thing was the lack of footprints. In fact when I showed Roy and Margaret the picture on my phone the child's face was there. Margaret saw it and fainted. Roy saw it too'.

'Yes I know they told us but for some strange reason, initially the child's face and now the whole of her has disappeared from your phone. Are you sure you didn't imagine the whole thing?'

'No of course I didn't. Look I showed Roy and Margaret and you've got the picture that I printed off'.

The discussion went on for about an hour at the end of which the Inspector stood up, stretched and asked if I would go with them to show where this meeting with Anna had taken place.

I got in the police car with the Inspector and lady sergeant and directed them to the point where Penny and I had started our walk into the woods.

Issuing a stream of instructions to the various members of the police team who'd followed in the other vehicles and who were now getting out of the police car and the Transit van the Inspector nodded at the dog van and shortly two police officers brought out two police dogs on leads, one a spaniel and the other an alsatian.

'Right sir. After you' instructed the Inspector, so I led off with him beside me and Sergeant Tara Boyson slightly behind us. Following us three, came the two officers with the dogs and behind them fanning out were several other policemen and women.

As we walked along I pointed out my tracks from yesterday and also where Penny had been charging about but in addition there were now more footsteps and dog prints as obviously other people had walked through the woods. Soon we reached the incline and as we got to a point where it was possible to see over the top. I stopped and said that this was where I had first seen the girl in the distance coming towards me. Then we walked on over the top and started down the other side to the point where I had talked to Anna.

'It was here, give or take an inch or two. Yes look that's where Penny flattened herself while we spoke. You remember I said that my dog seemed most distressed and you can see the mark she made in the snow when she laid down'.

The Inspector thanked me and then he and the Sergeant looked around in all directions before he took a document out of his pocket and opened it.

'This is a map of these woods and it shows where the police concentrated their search when they were looking for the child fourteen years ago. Interestingly it would seem that they only gave a relatively cursory search here in this area and for some reason appeared to spend most of their time on the other side of the wood. I gather that was because Anna's parents said that it was the area she often walked or played in. Right sir now will you please tell and show me, what you did after you finished talking to the girl?'

'I asked her if she needed any help and she said no. Actually she was very well spoken and polite and said no thank you, so then I watched her walk away the way I'd come and when she'd gone I carried on with my walk.

'Are you quite sure you spoke to her sir?' queried Tara Boyson looking directly at me.

'Yes quite sure'.

'You realise the girl we're talking about has been missing for fourteen years and would now be in her mid twenties?'

'Yes so I gather but the person to whom I spoke wasn't in her twenties but a school girl. I thought about twelve or thirteen. I believe she was twelve when she vanished.

'Yes she was' replied the Inspector. 'Now is there anything else that you can tell us sir?'

'No'.

He again looked closely at me then called some of the other police who'd been following us over to him. 'Bert I want this whole area searched from let's say fifty yards either side of the top of this incline. All along the track in both directions and say ten yards in on either side of it. Dogs, cameras, ground radar, the works. Got it?'

'Yes Gov' came the response as the officer concerned turned and walked back to his colleagues.

The Inspector then spoke to me. 'We're going to search the area again and see what we find, if anything. We've got much better search equipment and technology nowadays than they had fourteen years ago. Right sir I'll get an officer to walk back with you to your house but you can leave us to it now'.

'I'm fine to walk back on my own you know thanks'.

'Well if you're sure Mr. Rushworth'.

But back home I couldn't settle to anything. I'd briefed Becky on what had happened and what the police had said then I settled down at my desk alongside her, fired up my laptop and tried to do some work but I was unable to concentrate and later in the afternoon before it got dark I walked back to the area where I'd left the police.

Large areas of the track and surrounding areas had been dug. They were using a combination of manpower with picks and shovels, but they'd also brought in a small mini tracked digger like a miniature JCB as well as a small bulldozer.

The Inspector was talking on the phone but he waved when he saw me and beckoned me over to him. It really was a hive of activity because as well as the bulldozer, digger and the Range Rover there was another four wheel drive police pickup and also a Land Rover which had towed a kind of mobile tea bar, the sort you see in lay-bys beside main roads where several police officers in dungarees were queuing for hot food and drink to sustain their digging and searching efforts along the track.

'How are you getting on?' I asked.

'Well we're making progress but so far we've not found anything as yet. As you can see we've dug either side of the track about ten metres into the woods and I guess we've covered some fifty metres or so lengthwise but it is hard slow work and we've a lot more to go'.

'I assume you're searching for a body?'

'Yes we are' then he stared directly into my eyes. 'I just hope that we're not being played for fools. Wasting police time is an offence you know Mr Rushworth'.

'I know but I've told you what I saw and I told you the truth'.

'For your sake then I hope so sir, as what you described is odd to say the least. Very odd. To be honest I don't know whether you really saw anything sir?'

'Look how many times do I have to bloody well tell you' I snapped. 'I did. I'm not some sort of chap who gets a thrill out of misleading the police you know. And there's the little girl's parents, err Roy and Margaret isn't it? I mean last night when they came to our house they looked so desperately sad and yet at the same time somehow sort of hopeful. There's no way I want to add to their sorrow or distress'.

'All right sir'.

'So what do you think I saw?'

'I just don't know. Maybe it was the ghost of little Anna?'

'And her dog?'

'Uh huh and her dog'.

'You're not serious surely?'

'I've no idea sir but you say you saw the girl and there is something on that picture you printed off that warrants us to spend time and effort having a look'.

'Is there anything I can do?'

'No just leave it to us and I suggest you get home before it gets dark. They're setting up arc lights at this moment so we can continue to work on into and through the night. I've got another team coming in soon to relieve this lot. If we find anything I'll let you know'.

Much later Becky and I were thinking of going to bed when there was a knock on the door. Peering out of the window I saw a police car and Inspector Martin Lloyd and Sergeant Tara Boyson waiting outside our front door.

'Can we come in for a moment Mr Rushworth?' he asked when I opened the door to them.

'Sure' and leading the way inside I called out to Becky 'Darling it's the police again'.

Everyone said "hello" to each other then the Inspector drew himself up to his full height and squared his shoulders.

'I am here to tell you that we have found what appear to be the remains of a child and a dog buried close to where you saw ..... well whatever it was that you saw. An apparition, a ghost? I don't know but it is strange that what we have found is so close to where you saw what looked like Anna and her dog'.

I suddenly felt a bit faint and quickly sat down in the

chair. 'God God' I muttered. 'Do you know how they died?'

'No not at this stage. We've a lot more searching, examining and studying of the site and surrounding area to do. The pathology team have just arrived for an initial examination of the area and then when they've completed that they'll take the remains back to the mortuary for a thorough and detailed investigation of them. But I have to say that I am quite clear in my own mind that at long last we've found Anna and Rex and without your help we'd never have done that. We have just been and told Roy and Margaret about our discovery.

Now before we go I have one final question to ask you tonight sir. Where were you fourteen years ago at this time?'

'Crikey I've no idea?'

'Think if you will sir. It could be rather important for you?'

'Important for me? Why?'

'Well you see Mr Rushworth we don't now have an unsolved missing person enquiry but undoubtedly a murder investigation and so I will need to go back fourteen years to re-open the case and find out who did this to the girl and the dog? So where were you at the time she disappeared sir?'

'Fourteen years ago. So as it is two thousand and ten now, that would be nineteen ninety six and I was fifteen at that time therefore I would have been at home in Reading where my parents lived'.

'Would they be able to corroborate that for you sir?'

'No. My father died five years ago from a heart attack and my mother has Alzheimer's and is in a care home.

She doesn't even recognise me now! But I was born and brought up in Reading, well Twyford on the outskirts to be precise and I lived there until I left home at nineteen to go to Bristol University'.

'And after that sir?'

'After I graduated I lived in London for a while then moved to Norwich as my firm has its headquarters there. I met Becky in two thousand and five and we got together properly quite soon after that. In two thousand and seven we moved in together to a flat in Norwich and got married the following year. So that would have been two thousand and eight. We bought and moved here to this cottage last summer. There you are that's a synopsis of my life. Is there anything else that you want to know?'

'No not at this stage thank you sir. You have been most helpful'.

***

Two days later apart from confirming that Anna had been stabbed and strangled and the dog had been stabbed several times nothing else occurred. The police claimed that they were treating the matter as a "Cold Case" but unlike the tv shows on that subject where usually in an hour's programme a small team of four or five actors playing the parts of policemen, policewomen and forensic scientists easily solve cases that are many years old, in reality this didn't happen here.

At the request of the family the local vicar asked for and duly received dispensation from the Bishop for Anna and Rex to be buried together and so one month later on a dull wet morning I joined the large group of mourners as two small coffins were gently lowered to lie side by side in the dark cold earth.

***

Some months passed then Detective Inspector Martin Lloyd called at the cottage one evening just as Becky had finished feeding the twins to thank me for my assistance and to advise that although the case would being kept open, they were still completely mystified as to who had attacked and killed the little girl and her dog and unfortunately had no more leads to follow up.

He was like everyone else unable to explain what it was that I'd seen that day in January except to assume that it was some sort of ghost. As fortunately that element of the whole affair had been kept out of the press, then media interest in a fourteen year old dead child's body soon waned and by September the village had returned to forgetting about Anna and Rex and so did I, although from time to time I still had a strange feeling about what I'd seen that wintery afternoon.

CHAPTER 4

Next Christmas was a jolly affair with both Becky and my parents coming to us for Christmas Day and the six of us plus the twins who were now eleven months old had a great time especially the four grandparents who simply doted on the babies.

However when the festivities of Yuletide had gone I found myself constantly looking at diaries and the calendar as the sixteenth of January drew ever closer. There had been some snow but nothing like the previous year but on the specific afternoon exactly one year to the day and approximately the same time since I'd seen my apparition of the girl and dog, I called Penny and telling Becky that I wanted a walk, headed for the woods.

I'd not walked on that track again since that fateful day a year ago and I noted how this time it was different. Snow again lay around everywhere but it wasn't the very thick covering of snow that last year had blanketed everything so deeply. The ground was still quite uneven to the side of the track where the area had been dug and disturbed during and after the search for Anna and although the police, or more likely a contractor I guessed, had bulldozed everything back into place it just didn't look natural as it had the previous year.

As I came close to the point where the bodies had been found I could see that some ten yards in to the side of the track there was a small wooden cross and beside it a little flowerbed bordered with stones in which a few green shoots of bulbs were already peeking through the snow which was all around the area, untouched, unmarked and blanketing the ground in a beautiful carpet of undisturbed white.

I paused to look at the cross but after a moment of quiet contemplation, turned to look ahead up the track towards the top of the incline then twisted round to glance back behind me from where I had come.

It was then that I felt the presence, a kind of feeling that suddenly I wasn't alone. Penny obviously felt it too as her hackles rose and giving a series of low growls at the back of her throat she moved towards me flattening herself closer to the ground, just as she had last year.

As I turned my head there they were. Anna and Rex were standing beside the cross looking at me. Rooted to the spot and feeling the hairs on the back of my neck rise, I was unable to move or speak.

Suddenly the child spoke and said softly 'You helped them to find us'.

My mouth went completely dry but I managed to croak 'I'm glad that I did'.

'So are we because now we are in Heaven and at peace. Thank you'.

I squeezed my eyes tightly shut and shook my head quite unable to believe what I'd just witnessed, but when I opened my eyes again they'd gone. Whatever I'd seen or heard, if indeed I'd seen or heard anything and not just imagined it, was no longer there in front of me.

Tentatively I took a few paces forward towards the cross where they'd been standing but I could see nothing. A gentle breeze rustled the trees and shrubs, but there was definitely nothing else. Standing completely still, I carefully, slowly and very thoroughly looked around in all directions.

There was no child. No dog. Nothing apart from me and Penny. Except......?

Except that right there on the ground in front of me beside the cross at the precise point where moments ago I'd seen Anna and Rex standing were six clear footprints in the snow.

Two were child sized and alongside them were four dog paw prints.

THE END

Ghosts only exists for those that want to see them.
Holtei

It's a frightening thing ...
cameras make ghosts out of people.
Bob Dylon.

We are not human beings on a spiritual journey.
We are spiritual beings on a human journey.
Stephen R Covey.

ALICE WAS THAT REALLY YOU?
CHAPTER 1

I'd rented this cottage close to the Norfolk coast for six months so that I could concentrate on writing a book. It would be my first such venture and I was deliberately taking a career gap to achieve that.

Having always wanted to write a book but not only never finding the time to devote to it because of the demanding role that I had in the company as Operations Director, but also over the past two years initially trying to prop up my failing marriage and failing and then managing the deteriorating relationship with Sandy eventually leading to an acrimonious divorce, I felt I now needed a complete break.

My employer, a major food manufacturer, had been going through hard times in the market place and had called for volunteers for redundancy. I'd put up my hand and been accepted. Therefore with a substantial chunk of cash in the bank equivalent to almost two years salary I could afford to be out of the work place for some time.

So end of marriage and end of job. That was certainly the makings of a complete break with my past routine.

Through an agency I had rented out my apartment in Northampton for the time that I'd be away and then via the wonders of the internet I found this little cottage in Norfolk. Having finalised the arrangements I took myself off for a luxury two week holiday in Barbados returning relaxed, suntanned, happy and at peace with myself to settle into the cottage.

My plan was to devote the six months to writing and then at the end I intended to spend the next few months job hunting until I found something that I thought would suit me. I knew it was a risk and that at the end of the process I might wind up without any job, but at thirty five I was confident that my track record which was good and the fact that I'd often been approached or headhunted before but had always said no would stand me in good stead. I knew I was on several head-hunters books and I felt sure that when the time was right I could, hopefully without too much difficulty, reactivate their interest to find me a good job. Well that was the plan. Time would tell if it worked out.

For the first couple of days at the cottage I didn't write at all. I didn't even fire up the laptop but got up late, ate some cereals, toast and fresh fruit as I was determined to also use this time to get fit and healthy eating was part of that plan. The cottage was fully equipped so after I'd eaten I cleared the breakfast table, loaded the dishwasher then went for a brisk walk, even jogging for a small part of it. That was something that I hadn't done for years and although I can't say that I enjoyed it and preferred walking, nevertheless I realised that by making part of my daily walk into a jog I'd be helping my intention of getting fit and so I decided to do that every day. Short jogs to start with and then longer sections.

Located about a quarter of a mile inland from the actual sea I had lots of choices of route to walk. Along the seashore, marshes and sand dunes, or inland across fields and through country lanes or tracks. I'd bought an Ordnance Survey map of the area and so was able to plot and follow routes off the beaten track.

After my walk when I got back I took a shower then with a mug of herbal tea in hand instead of my usual strong black coffee, another surrender to getting fit and healthy, I made my way onto the patio which was to the side of the building.

I sat looking at the scene of trees, shrubs and open fields that lay before me letting my mind ramble around several themes and ideas for a book that had been forming but lying dormant for the last three to four years.

For lunch I just ate fruit and for an evening meal I'd stocked up on some microwave meals because I am no cook, but I'd tried to make the selection of those that I'd bought vary between healthy and tasty.

I wasn't going to be a total goody goody about my getting fit, so I'd laid in a decent supply of beer, lager, wine and some malt whisky. It was just that I was going to be more abstemious than had been the case for the last couple of years.

There was a pub further down the village and I'd already been in and said hello. The landlord Roy and his wife Rita were a cheerful happy couple who calling themselves the two R's were originally from the Midlands but had lived in Norfolk for the past fifteen years and almost thought themselves as locals but had only moved to this village and bought the pub three years ago.

The pub itself was traditional, served food which I knew I'd be enjoying from time to time when microwave meals waned in excitement, and had a nice selection of beers including regular guest brews. It was warm, friendly and welcoming, just what a village pub should be and for that reason it was very popular.

It also had one other advantage because as well as Roy and Rita there was a girl called Shelley but most people seemed to just call her Shel. She divided her time between serving behind the bar and doing some waitressing as the two R's had established a good reputation for their wholesome 'pub grub' type of food and thus had a few tables to one side of the bar. Shel who was in her early twenties was pretty, lively, cheeky and fun with a nice neat waist, a cute bum and a lovely pair of breasts which she obviously didn't mind displaying as most of her blouses, jumpers and shirts seemed to be extremely low cut and ably showed off her more than ample charms.

My problem with the potential book was whether to write a story based on my business experience but who would be interested in a life that had involved running production lines and then eventually whole factories? Or should I write a mystery. Maybe a "who-dun-it"? Alternatively perhaps I ought to pen a raunchy story of love and passion perhaps featuring a boob flashing bar maid like Shel?

I really couldn't decide, but in the end it was events that decided for me what I should write.

***

It was on the third day of my self imposed exile that I made up my mind, walked indoors fired up the laptop, had a large sip from my mug of camomile tea took a deep breath and typed CHAPTER 1.

It looked good but half an hour later that was still all that was sitting there on the page until eventually, slowly at first but then with increasing confidence and fluidity I found that the words started to flow in a trickle to start with but then intensifying, if not to a torrent at least to a steady stream.

I was going to write about my life so far. My childhood upbringing in London, my parents, schooling, my time at university, entry into industry and my career climb to date. After all even though I'd taken a career break I'd had a successful business life until now and making the position of Operations Director for a major company five years ago then aged just thirty, had been quite an achievement and something of which I was extremely proud.

What I wasn't sure about at the moment though was whether to include the details of my marriage which had started so happily but descended into mutual dislike, acrimony, constant rows and eventual almost hatred of each other. The only good thing was that there were no children to suffer from the wreck although maybe if there had been we might not have broken up.

I typed all morning and by the time I broke off at lunch time I'd made good progress and had written over three thousand words. As I'd read somewhere that Ian Fleming when writing the James Bond books used to try and produce two thousand words a day, I thought that for my first day's work I'd done pretty well.

Stretching I stood and wandered into the kitchen and choosing a selection of fruit moved back to the sitting room plonking down onto the surprisingly comfortable settee, dragged a padded footstool in front of me propped up my feet and relaxed as I ate, satisfied with what I now saw as the first real morning's work for my writing project.

So the pattern of my days as a potential future bestselling author progressed.

***

Some days I wrote quite a lot but other days I struggled and perhaps only produced a few hundred words. However after about a month I was pleased with my progress and had some forty thousand words written which if turned into a book would create a finished article somewhere between a quarter and a third the size of a normal paperback. So although I was doing ok, there was a long way to go before this book was finished. Still I had another four months remaining from my personally set six month target time to complete my masterpiece. Financially I was ok, as I wasn't spending much money. Just the rental of the cottage, food and drink, an occasional meal at the pub and a regular nightly pint, where I enjoyed the pub's atmosphere as well as staring at Shel's lovely boobs.

Surprisingly I was also enjoying the solitude and my relatively simple unhurried existence which made such a change from the hassle and hustle of my former life running high speed automated manufacturing lines in an extremely demanding timescale to meet constantly increasing and tougher production and output targets.

Yes all was well with my life, except for one thing. I was starting to miss female company. Not just to talk to, but more importantly in bed. The simple fact was that I was getting horny and frequent nightly leering down Shel's low cut fronts didn't help!

I'd always enjoyed a healthy and fairly active sex life ever since I had first discovered just what a man and a woman could do with each other. Before getting married I'd had lots of relationships ranging from one night stands to some longish liaisons, but after I'd met Sandy I was faithful to her and I believe she was to me. The reason was simple because as well as actually believing in the sanctity of marriage, Sandy was bloody good in bed, constantly innovative, always ready for a good bonk and she worked hard to make it good for me as well as herself. Indeed even in the final stages of our marriage breakdown we still shagged away like it was going out of fashion. After all it wasn't the sex that had gone wrong - it was everything else and she needed sex as much as I did!

But now it was going on for three months since I'd got my leg over and I was certainly starting to, if not feel desperate, at least experience some real frustration and I knew that I was going to have to do something about it. And soon! After all I'd come away to be quiet and secluded in order to write a book, not to turn into a celibate monk!

CHAPTER 2

The next night in the pub I asked Shel for some recommendations for clubs and she gave me the names and locations of two in Norwich so the following day after finishing writing around lunch time and going for a really long afternoon walk in addition to my pre breakfast trot I decided I'd venture into the Norwich that night.

Back at the cottage I made something to eat then had a leisurely bath, changed and around ten was in the City, found somewhere to park and checked out the two clubs and they were both as you'd expect.

Noisy, brash, crowded, overpriced drinks, booming music. I just had a couple of drinks in the first but in the second perhaps loosened up by a third drink I chatted up some girls but to be honest there wasn't one there with whom I thought I'd enjoy any sort of relationship. Sure there were a few I'd happily bed, and a couple made it perfectly clear that if that's what I wanted then it wouldn't be a problem but I didn't think that was really what I wanted. Certainly I wasn't looking to start any sort of proper or permanent relationship so what was I looking for?

'Come on' I told myself, 'you came tonight looking for sex and there are some here that will more than willingly provide it so stop being too choosy and prevaricating with yourself and just get on with it!'

So I did!

Alice was tall, articulate, pretty face, nice figure, long shapely legs most of which were on show as her skirt barely covered her knickers and after we'd chatted and smooch danced, clearly up for it.

Having stressed to me that she didn't usually go home with men on a first date and after discussing where we both lived; she here in the City, me twenty five miles away, and having further informed me that she didn't like sex in a car as it was too cramped it was a mutual no-brainer of a decision that we should go to her place so with lots of exaggerated hugging and cheek kissing of her two female companions with whom she'd come out this evening she promised to call them later "after we'd finished" as she so delicately put it!

We left the club together. Not only was I pleased to have succeeded in achieving my ambition for the night but I was also very glad that I wasn't having to drive far as really I'd had too much to legally get behind the wheel but I was sure if I was careful we'd be alright.

Alice held onto my arm as we walked to the multi-story car park and as soon as I'd blipped the key to unlock the car, I held open the passenger door for her which she acknowledged with a smile as she sat then carefully swung those wonderful legs into the car during which I noticed that she very primly kept her knees tightly together although I hoped that it wasn't going to be long before they were spread nice and wide with me in between them!

Moments later I was behind the wheel and turning to her leaned forward and went for a little kiss but I promptly discovered that Alice didn't do little kisses! She pulled my head to hers and kissed me back hard, passionately and intensely forcing her tongue deep into my mouth. We stayed in the car locked together for quite some time, letting our lips and our tongues get properly acquainted. She also didn't object when I squeezed her breasts, but when I popped open the top button of her dress and tried to undo some more so that I could get my fingers inside her bra she took hold of my probing hand and stopped me.

'Hey whoa hang on. You're not getting 'em out here. Wait till we get back to my place then you can have as much fun with my boobies as you want'.

Pulling away I nodded and asked for directions to her flat. With a nice smile as she did up the loosened buttons she said it wasn't far, then fastening her seat belt sat upright and directed me as we left the car park.

She was right it took a little less than ten minutes but on the way I was both surprised and delighted when she ran a hand up and down my thigh a few times before letting it rest in my crotch where she squeezed me a couple of times before taking my zip which she slid down and started to feel around inside.

'I hope I'm not going to be disappointed with what you've got in here Russ?' she giggled.

'Well I've never had any complaints before'.

'That's good but I'm a rather hard to please and particular girl you know' she laughed doing a little more rummaging during which her fingers didn't actually venture inside my boxers but they did spend a minute or two rubbing up and down my prick from the outside which inevitably started it erecting.

'Umm now that feels promising' she chuckled removing her hand and then this time using both hands zipped me up as we drove along every now and then leaning over to lick my ear and kiss my cheek.

'I think we're going to have a lot of fun' she whispered once again putting her hand on my crotch and this time leaving it there. Fortunately it wasn't long after that before we were pulling into a visitor's space outside a five storey block of what were obviously new apartments.

I got out and went round to open her door, grinned when she said it was nice to be with a gentleman, and enjoyed watching those lovely legs as they emerged from the car, this time not tightly clamped together at the knees thus affording me a quick but rather nice flash of white panty. I locked the car behind us then holding her hand walked with her to the outer door of the apartment block which she opened with a swipe card, followed her across the hallway to the lift and up to the fourth floor where after a short walk down a corridor she stopped outside a door, fumbled around in her bag, found a key, unlocked and pushed open the door and led the way inside.

'Would you like a drink?' she queried.

'Err well if you're having one that would be great, thanks'.

'Don't have to you know? If you want to go straight to bed and get on with it then that's fine by me' and pouting she sashayed across the room to me and wrapping her arms around my neck kissed me again forcing my teeth apart with her tongue and turning the kiss into a distinctly erotic and passionate event as she slowly started to push her crotch against me.

I responded by pressing myself back against her conscious that she must be able to feel my erection starting up again. Whether she could or not I don't know but what I did know was that she reacted straight away by now starting to grind her hips from side to side while at the same time shoving her own crotch area forward and really pressing against me as she slid her hands around my waist then down to clasp my bottom and heaving me against herself. Moments later she slid firstly one hand and then the other inside the waistband of my trousers and my pants and started to gently rake her fingernails up and down the skin of my buttocks. We continued like that for a little while, kissing and pressing together while she scratched my bum cheeks before she eased her body and then her head away.

'Well now which would you prefer? Would you like to have a drink, or would you rather have me?'

Actually I would really have loved a beer but I think her offering of a choice was only teasing and not wanting to dampen her obvious willing ardour I replied 'You'.

'Good that's what I wanted to hear you to say. Come on then the bedroom's this way'.

'And if I'd chosen the beer?'

'Oh in that case I'd have cut your balls off!'

'I wouldn't have been a lot of good to you this evening if you'd done that'.

'Oh I'd have shagged you first then cut them off very slowly one at a time ensuring that I inflicted the most incredible pain onto you while I did it' and her laugh rang around the apartment which was tiny but neat, orderly, immaculately clean and comprised a small hallway leading into this main room at the far end of which was a kitchen area. Up two steps to a little landing which led to the bathroom to the left and to her bedroom to the right.

As soon as we were in the bedroom we kissed again then easing back she took my hands and lifting them to her chest advised '*Now* you are more than welcome to undo the buttons'.

I did as suggested also dropping a kiss onto the side of her neck as I eased the little dress off her shoulders and down past her waist. I knelt down to help her slip it over her feet as turning her back to me she kicked off her shoes to assist its removal. I plonked a kiss on each of her buttocks which were covered by her pretty white lacy panties of which I'd briefly seen the front flash a few minutes earlier.

Standing up again I unclipped her bra and ran my tongue along the mark in the middle of her back made by the bra strap. Turning round to face me she smiled as she lifted the shoulder straps and slipped the bra down her arms and off to expose her breasts to my eager gaze, and although her dress had been incredibly short showing most of her legs, the front had been quite high necked and so this was the first chance that I'd had to see them. I'd guessed that they were not insubstantial as they had seemed generously sized behind her dress but then you never know do you? It could have all been silicone chicken fillet padding! Fortunately it wasn't.

Immediately they were free from the bra and wobbling slightly as she moved she took each of her nipples between her thumbs and fingers and teased herself before lifting up the breasts themselves and holding them out to me. 'Here you are this is what you wanted a little while ago in the car park wasn't it?'

I took hold of them and started to massage as she whispered 'Oh now that's really nice' and it wasn't long before I lowered my lips to her nipples where she allowed me to kiss, suck and gently chew before she pushed my head away and reaching out to my shirt quickly unbuttoned and tugged it off, dropping it on to a side chair.

Now it was her turn to kneel and my trousers were soon off and joined the shirt and as I hurriedly tugged off my socks I saw that Alice had moved to the bed and was lying on her side watching me as I walked over and sat down.

'You are sure about this aren't you?' I asked.

'Uh huh oh yes I am quite sure' and I watched as she slid her panties off and handed them to me. 'There we are now bold, completely bare and ready for you' she grinned stretching her arms and legs wide. 'Like what you see?'

'Yes you are very beautiful' I said quietly and truthfully as I started down at her nude body.

'Thank you. Right mister, now get these off' she instructed tapping my boxers 'and put this on' and she handed me a condom foil. As I covered myself I noticed her slip one hand below her pubic bush and from the finger movements I guessed she was massaging herself as she lay watching me until I naked but protected clambered onto the bed as she wrapped her arms around my neck and encouraged me to clamber on top of her to make love.

Immediately I felt her legs wrap themselves around my waist as she humped herself against me in time to my rhythm with her and then as we both got into our stride I felt her nails scrape down my back as she started to become more abandoned in her lovemaking.

Alice was obviously an experienced lover and although it wasn't the best sex that I'd ever had, it certainly ranked up there along with some of the better sessions. However I couldn't help thinking that if it was this good on our first time then given a few more sessions together it could become really quite something special.

Climaxing almost simultaneously, she rather noisily but at least it proved I'd made her come; gradually we both calmed down and cuddled closely together stroking and kissing tenderly.

'Hey you' she said softly looking up at me and smiling 'that was pretty damn good. Thanks'.

'The pleasure was all mine'.

'Well let's agree to share the pleasure. Now do you want that beer?'

'Only if I get your assurance that my balls safe?' I laughed quietly.

'Ah now there's a question isn't it? Let's see' she chuckled pushing me aside, then leaning forward and lifting my prick out of the way she put her head on one side and studied them for a moment before murmuring 'oh yes I think they are quite safe' then to my great delight she leant down, kissed each one, kissed my now partly flaccid prick before running an outstretched lovely pink tongue up the length of me, looked up and grinned then rolling out of bed picked the used condom off the duvet and walked out of the room returning a few minutes later with two already opened bottles of a posh Italian beer, having stopped off in the bathroom on the way back as I'd heard the flush. Handing one to me she said 'Cheers' and raised her own to her lips and drank.

'Cheers' I replied as I took a deep swig then I leaned forward and licked her nipples.

'Umm that's nice. I'd think I'd like you to carry on doing that for a while please' she whispered as pulling my head to her chest she settled back against the headboard and started stroking my hair while every now and then taking a little sip of her beer. While I continued to carry out her request by dutifully licking and gently chewing her nipples which responded by hardening a little, she picked up her mobile, paged through and pressed the call button.

'Hi you' she said to someone 'yes I'm fine. In fact I'm better than fine. I'm good, really good'. There was a pause as she listened then with a chuckle she continued 'Yes he's here right beside me. Russ say hello to my best friend Isobel' and she held the phone to my ear.

'Hello Isobel'.

'Hello Russ. Now are you being nice to my friend Alice?' said the disembodied voice.

'Yes very nice to her and she's being very nice to me as well'.

'Is she, well that's great. So where are you?'

'She wants to know where we are' I whispered to Alice as I covered the mouthpiece.

'Oh Izzy you silly mare, we're in bed calming down after making love but now he's being a good boy and licking my nips for me. Wherever did you think we'd be?' Alice called out leaning towards the phone.

'You dirty pair' chuckled the phone voice as I put it back to my ear.

'No it wasn't dirty, it was lovely' I replied.

'Good for you, now can I speak to Alice again please?'

Saying yes and handing the phone back to her I wriggled up, leaned back against the headboard and sipped at my beer as Alice chatted to her friend.

I was struck by the incongruity of the situation.

Here we were. Two people who'd never met before this evening, had spent about half an hour chatting in the club, enjoyed two or three smoochy dances and then left together, come back to her apartment, jumped into bed and less than ten minutes ago we were furiously rutting away at each other. Now she was sitting up in bed naked, chatting to her friend Izzy while I sat alongside her alternating between sipping a beer, licking her nipples, belly button and pubic hair while enjoying looking at her rather nice naked body.

My musing was brought to a fairly abrupt halt as still holding the mobile to her ear but with a puzzled expression she pushed me a little away from her then ran a hand over my chest, looked at me and said into the phone 'Yep nice abs' then as her hand trailed down to my belly she added 'and a great six pack'. Basking in the compliments I was surprised by her sudden burst of laughter as she put her hand on my prick and stretched it out.

'It's not circumcised and I'd say it's maybe a little bit bigger than average' then putting on a serious expression as she gently tugged and stretched my foreskin out added 'but not a lot. However he knows how to use it alright' and she laughed again.

Seeing my bemused expression she twisted round, leant down and gave a long slow lick along the length of me then changed hands with the phone to move it to her free ear as she rested her head on the top of my thighs and started to entangle a forefinger in my pubic hair. Looking up she blew a kiss to me.

'Izzy wants to know if you're going to stay the night' Alice asked still holding the phone in one hand while untangling her finger and moving it to the end of my prick where she teased me with her fingernail.

'I'd like to if that's ok with you?'

'He says he'd like to if it's ok with me' and then as she listened for a moment she eased my foreskin down with a little jerk before sliding it back into place then looked up at me.

'Izzy says that I should let you as long as you screw me again before we go to sleep. No screw. No stay'.

'It will be my pleasure' I replied quietly but meaningfully then leaning towards the phone I called out loudly 'Thank you Izzy'.

'He said thank you. Did you hear? A very polite man is our Russ' Alice chortled. 'Right Izzy I'm really sorry you haven't pulled so far tonight. I thought that tall blonde haired bloke you were chatting to at the bar looked as though he had the hots for you. No? Really? Gay? You're kidding me? Honestly? Wow what a waste!' then looking at her watch she added 'still there's a couple of hours yet before the club shuts so go on girl, brush your hair and make it shine, re-do your makeup, stick your tits out, wiggle your bum and get pulling. Me I'm going to make the most of what I've got right here. Bye and hey, call me later ok?'

'Can I get another beer?' I asked as she wriggled up the bed and put the phone on the bedside table.

'Sure. Fridge in kitchen area of the main room. Second shelf. Help yourself'.

'Do you want another?'

'No. At least not a beer but I definitely want another of what we had together a few minutes ago' and pouting sexily she blew a kiss then calling out 'don't be long Russ will you?' she slid down the bed to lie on her back with one knee pulled up.

I came back with the beer, kissed her raised knee, clambered onto the bed and slowly sipped the beer as we talked a little about each other. I discovered she worked for one of the big companies in Norwich in their accounts department specialising in chasing up outstanding debts. She was fascinated to learn that I was taking a kind of sabbatical from work to write my book.

'So if it's all about your life will I be in it?' she queried.

'Maybe. I haven't got that far yet'.

We went on talking for a while then reaching into the bedside cupboard she produced another condom, moved to sit on my lower legs and feet and using her hands and lips soon brought me to a fully erect state. Rolling the condom onto me she wriggled up my body then slowly lowered herself down onto me and we made love with her happily and enthusiastically bouncing around on top.

Eventually we went to sleep and I'd almost dropped off when Alice's mobile beeped to indicate receipt of a text. Sleepily I watched her reach out, pick it up and stare at the little screen.

'Ah she's pulled. Good for Izzy. She doesn't often miss out' and with a contented sigh she cuddled into me. 'Hey by the way I have to be work at eight in the morning so I need to leave here by just after seven thirty which means I get up at six thirty so they'll be no long lie in for you tomorrow Russ. Nor will there be any action with this' she added feeling for my prick which having found she gently squeezed.

'That's a shame' I muttered.

'Umm but there simply won't be time I'm afraid. I can't be doing with all that quick humping and bumping early on a work morning. Now if it was Saturday or Sunday tomorrow and we could have a lie in, then that might be different. But it isn't. Sorry babe. Some other time eh?' and giving me another quick squeeze she let go of me, leaned over to kiss my shoulder and whispered 'night night'.

We were both soon fast asleep.

CHAPTER 3

Next morning as soon as her alarm clock shrilled at six thirty Alice rolled out of bed, leaned down, muttered 'Morning babe', gave me a little kiss, headed for the shower, returning to the bedroom about twenty minutes later wrapped in a large towel and sat at her dressing table to dry her hair saying over her shoulder as she switched on the hairdryer 'Don't forget I leave at seven thirty sharp and so that means that you do as well Russ'.

Somewhat sleepily I grunted 'Ok' then watched as she dried and brushed her long tresses until she was happy with them before opening a drawer and extracting a pair of cream panties, slid them up her legs, then took what looked like a matching bra and fitted her nice sized shapely breasts into it. Seeing me watching her she grinned and struck a pose with her hands on her hips and thrust her crotch forward towards me, before spinning slowly round in a circle, pausing briefly to bend her knees and waggle her knicker clad bum at me then with a laugh and a pouted kiss she opened a wardrobe door and extracted a pair of smart dark grey business trousers, followed by a pale blue blouse which she held up, studied critically, grunted, put it back and walked over to a chest of drawers and extracted a dark green jumper which she pulled over her head and smoothed down around herself.

'You need the bathroom?' she queried looking at me still in bed 'as if you do you'd better get a move on? I usually just have a slice of toast. Will that do you too?'

I said it would be fine as I sat up and swung my legs out of bed. Not having any shaving or washing gear with me, I went and stood under the shower and let it pound me for a minute or two before getting out and finding a warm towel I dried myself and wandered back into the bedroom where I pulled on the clothes I was wearing last night. Dressed I went to the sitting room where Alice sitting on one of two high stools in the kitchen area smiled and pointed to some slices of toast which she'd just taken out of the toaster.

'I've got jam, honey, marmalade and there's some cheese or ham if you like to go continental?'

'Honey will be fine thanks' and soon I was sitting on the other stool buttering then spreading the thick produce of bees onto two slices of toast which I munched happily as she poured me a glass of orange juice. Standing with a piece of toast in one hand she asked 'Tea or coffee?'

'Neither. The juice will be ok for me thanks'.

Nodding she slid back up onto her stool, picked up the rest of her toast and soon we'd both finished. The time was seven twenty five.

'Look thanks Alice. I *really* enjoyed last night, all of it'.

'Yes so did I. It was good wasn't it? Right, now it's time we were going' and sliding off the stool she quickly collected the plates and glasses, loaded them into the dishwasher, looked around, hunted in her handbag to find a lipstick then peering in the hallway mirror carefully coloured her lips, pouted and made a moue, before sliding the handbag over her arm and picking up her mobile phone and car keys, turned to me and with a grin said 'Right come on it's time to go. Might see you again sometime Russ' and headed towards the door.

'Would you like to meet up again?'

'Maybe?'

'Shall I call you? What's your number?'

'No but give me yours and I'll call you'.

So I did but as we stood in the lift I again asked her for her phone number. She looked hard at me then as the lift got to the ground floor and the doors opened she sighed. 'Alright but don't pester me. Now have you got a piece of paper?' she asked taking a pen out of her bag.

'Here write it on this' and I held out my hand palm upwards and with a shrug she did so pressing surprisingly hard with the ballpoint pen but at least there was her phone number.

'Thank you'.

'Pleasure. Right see you around. Bye Russ' and with a smile, a peck of a kiss on my lips followed by a careful wipe over of them with her forefinger to remove any trace of pink lipstick and a wave she walked over to an obviously very new white Fiat 500, unlocked it and slid behind the wheel. I watched as she started the engine and then drove carefully out of the car park giving me another wave and blowing me a kiss she was gone.

I went to my car and drove back to my little cottage reflecting on my date with Alice. Passionate and very willing last night but this morning she was polite, friendly yet quite stand-offish about another date. Ah well such is life. However not only had it been a good shag last night but at least I knew where she worked and I had her phone number.

Back at the cottage I copied her phone number from my hand into my mobile, stripped off last night's clothes and walked around naked for a little while trying to decide what to do then having made up my mind I had a shower my second in a matter of an hour or so, shaved, dressed, made some coffee, sat at the window and looked over the marshes in front of the cottage and thought about my book.

Soon I had fired up the laptop and was busily engrossed in writing although every now and then Alice crept into my mind as I saw her face but especially her body as I'd watched her teasing me while getting dressed this morning.

***

I wrote all day instead of just the morning and when I went to bed that night I was not only pleased with the progress that I'd made but also I kept thinking about Alice and seeing her pretty face and nice body in my mind.

Every couple of weeks after that, I went into Norwich to various restaurants for a meal which made a pleasant change from the local pub or my own efforts at cooking. Also several times I went to night clubs where I chatted up girls and surprisingly often managed to pull and as a result I saw the inside of several female bedrooms in a variety of flats, houses, bedsits and apartments.

I saw Alice again on four other evening occasions. Once at the club where we originally met; once when she agreed to go out for supper with me to an Italian restaurant in the City; once at another club and once at a pub karaoke night. Each time she proved to be lively, vivacious and good company and at the end of the evening I went back to her little apartment with her where I had a wildly enjoyable hour or so shagging her. Three times she wouldn't let me to stay the night and so I left somewhere between eleven thirty and one in the morning. But once it was a Saturday evening that we met up and so when we got back to her apartment after we'd shagged twice not only did she let me stay for the whole night, but as she didn't have to get up early for work next day we lazed around in bed in the morning passing the time by eating toast and drinking juice and coffee in bed interspersed with another couple of bloody good shags.

***

It was about three months after we'd first met when one morning I rang her to try and fix a date but she said that she couldn't see me again.

'Why not? Come on Alice we get on well and have fun together?'

'Yes we do but I'm afraid the answer is still no'.

'Look have I upset you in some way?'

'No Russ it's not that but it's just not possible'.

'But why? I don't understand?'

She sighed deeply. 'Because my husband gets back tomorrow'.

'Your *husband?* God I didn't know you were married?'

'Well I am. He's in the army and been in Afghanistan but his battalion gets back tomorrow and I'm going to meet him. He'll be living in married quarters so I'll move back there to be with him'.

'Good grief. I'm sorry but you weren't wearing a ring and you never said'.

'Of course not. If I'd worn a wedding ring would you have picked me up?'

'No probably not' I admitted.

'Well there you are then. I love Jerry but I can't go

all that time without, well shall we say without a man, so when he's posted abroad I move out of the married quarters as they are really crummy and into that little apartment that I rent. Jerry knows nothing about it.

I have to be really careful as the other wives and girlfriends at the married quarters are a really nosey bunch of old crones but they think I've gone back to my parents as I have to give them some sort of reason for disappearing.

When he's away then I go out and enjoy myself but when he's home I'm the loyal dutiful wife. So sorry honey and it's been great fun with you but it's over for a few months at least as he'll be based here in the UK for the next six months, maybe longer, before he's off abroad again. Look I've got your number but give me the address of the cottage you're renting. Then when he's posted away again and if you are still in Norfolk, although I guess you might have finished your book and returned to wherever by then, but if not then I'll call you or come over and see you. As you're not working nine to five in an office I might just turn up and surprise you. Hey by the way am I in your book yet?'

'You will be' I laughed. 'Right well I guess this is goodbye for now then. Been great knowing you' and I rang off.

Now that was a real surprise. Well shock really I guess. Married and husband in the army. Blimey!

CHAPTER 4

Work on the book was proceeding well but after another month I'd come to a bit of an impasse. Writer's block I guess they call it. I was happy with what I'd written so far and I knew how the book was going to end but I was really struggling to find the link between where I'd *got* to and where I wanted to *get* to.

I slogged away for several days but wrote little and it was really beginning to bug me. Eventually I decided to have a break and go away so I rang my brother who lives at Wokingham in Berkshire, explained my predicament and asked if I could come and stay for a few days.

Lawrence is good fun and so is his wife Natalie. They have two kids, boisterous boys aged nine and eleven and they are a happy family. Natalie works part time in a building society branch in nearby Bracknell and Lawrence is an engineering draughtsman and always involved with complicated new construction of bridges, tunnels or some similar such massive building projects.

I arrived with them on Thursday and left on Sunday after lunch. The break did me good and I thought that I'd been able to clear my mind and could now see a way forward for the book.

Once I got clear of the M4 and M11 and left the Sunday afternoon traffic behind, it became a pleasant drive back to the north Norfolk coast and as I bowled along I was looking forward to returning to the cottage and making a start again on the book. I decided as I drove that I would get going again this evening as I wanted to start the creative thoughts flowing again and break the log-jam that had been there before.

Nearing the coast and turning into the little lane down which about three quarters of a mile along my cottage was located it was a surprise as I drove down a small incline and then round a sharp bend to see in the distance a young woman standing in the road waving at me.

She looked to be in some sort of distress as her waving and walking into the centre of the road was clearly designed to make me stop. I slowed to a halt and put down the window of the car.

To my amazement when she came over to the car I saw it was Alice. Her hair was tousled; there was a tear in her dress and she had a long deep cut to her cheek from which blood was slowly oozing down her face.

I jumped out of the car and my immediate thought was that her husband must have found out about her being unfaithful and had beaten her up and for some reason she'd come to me for help.

'Hi Alice. Whatever's the matter?'

'I've had an accident. My car went off the road' she said in a dull flat voice.

'Are you hurt?'

'Not really'.

'Was there anyone else with you?'

'No just me'.

'Whatever were you doing here?'

'I've come to see you. You gave me your address. Jerry has gone back abroad and I wanted to see you again'.

'I thought he was going to be here for months'.

'He was originally but the silly sod volunteered for some special mission and so now he's gone. We had a row about it but he went anyway. Yesterday. I felt so miserable that I wanted cheering up so I drove up here to come and find you'. Her voice was quiet and again I thought it sounded bland, quiet and monotone, definitely not her usual bright bubbly cheery sound.

'Well that's great. Now what about your car? Do you need help with it?'

'No'.

'But if it's off the road following your crash ....'

'It's fine where it is' she interrupted. 'Don't worry about it. Leave it. It's me that needs comforting. Please?'

'Get in' and I helped her into the passenger seat noticing as I held her arm that she felt very cold.

It was only a matter of a few more minutes before we pulled up in front of Badgers Holt as the cottage was named and she duly "oo-ed" and "aah-ed" as it was really very pretty and in the early autumn late afternoon sunshine looked like a picture postcard of a traditional Norfolk cottage.

I led the way indoors. She refused a hot drink and said that she just wanted to rest so I took her upstairs to the bedroom, pulled back the duvet, sat her down, saw that she didn't have any shoes on which I'd not noticed before, and suggested that she lie down. She did so then I pulled the duvet up and tucked it around her body which still felt bitterly cold. Turning onto her side for a moment she curled up into a ball and hugged herself with her damaged cheek resting down onto the pillow. After a moment or two she turned over onto her other side and lay still for a while before twisting to lie on her back.

'I'm cold' she whispered her eyes staring at me 'come and warm me up'.

'Look you've had a shock. You need to rest'.

'I can rest later ...... for ever if necessary' and although her voice was still lacklustre she smiled as she held up her arms, but it was a sad smile I thought. Previously when I'd been with her she'd always been a lively, full of fun, exciting, happy person but now she was quite the opposite. Dreary and jaded. Her eyes which usually sparkled and twinkled were dull, expressionless and had an almost vacant look.

Not being sure of the right treatment for shock, nevertheless she was attractive and offering herself to me, so on the theory that a good bonk might take her mind off whatever had happened to her and as she'd said that no-one else was involved and the car didn't matter I grinned and walking over to the windows pulled the curtains closed then quickly stripped off.

Approaching the bed I flicked the duvet aside and was surprised to see she was now completely naked. Odd as I hadn't heard, noticed or been conscious that she'd been undressing still with a shrug I climbed into the bed, pulled her to me and shivered as she was freezing cold.

'Warm me up' she whispered.

I rolled on top and wondered aloud about a condom as I didn't have any at the cottage because this was the first time I'd brought a girl back here for sex.

'Don't worry you'll be fine' she whispered and pulled me into her. The lovemaking was good and she seemed to have warmed up as we humped away at each other but when we'd finished and I cuddled her into my side I noticed that once again she felt cold.

We drifted off to sleep together and I hoped that the heat of my body together with the duvet which I'd tucked around us both would soon warm up her chilly body.

When I awoke a little later there was no sign of her. Assuming she was in the bathroom I lay still for a few minutes but I couldn't hear any sounds from her so I wandered along the landing to see if she was alright but she wasn't in there. Nor was she in the spare bedroom, the one that I didn't use. Going downstairs there was simply no sign of her anywhere. She'd gone.

Shrugging I went back upstairs and got dressed then returned downstairs and had a walk around the garden and then right round the cottage outside. I looked in the garage and the two outbuildings which were full of gardening things but of Alice there was simply no sign. She'd completely vanished.

I have to say that I thought it was very odd that she'd just slipped away without saying goodbye, or thank you or indeed anything!

Back upstairs again I had a shower paying special attention to washing my genitals as we'd made love without a condom, something that I only rarely did with strange women but after a thorough soaping I dried, dressed, went down to the kitchen and fixed myself an omelette and microwave chips which I washed down with a glass of red wine. Afterwards I got out the laptop and wrote until gone midnight during which I drank the rest of the bottle of wine which certainly helped my writing thoughts!

CHAPTER 5

Next morning after I got up I went for my usual pre-breakfast walk, came back and had something to eat and then on an impulse looked up Alice's phone number and dialled but it went straight to voicemail. I listened to her voice for a moment or two as she said that she was unable to take the call and to please leave a message. For some reason I didn't.

Something was continuing to nag me though about yesterday's encounter with her so following a good morning spent writing I made a mug of soup for my lunch after which I decided to go for another walk and this time for some reason I headed back to where I'd picked Alice up yesterday afternoon.

As I ambled round the bend approaching the spot, a man looked at me and held up his hand to stop me and called out 'Hang on there for a minute mate'.

Behind him a breakdown truck was parked across the lane completely blocking it and the narrow grass verges on both sides. Another man was in the process of operating the winch hauling a white Fiat 500 slowly out of the undergrowth towards the low loader part of the truck.

I walked over and spoke him.

'Hi there'.

'Sorry to hold you up mate' he said 'but won't be too long now. Just got to winch the car onto the truck and tie it down then we'll be out of your way'.

'No problem. I'm in no hurry. What happened? Do you know?'

'Yea shocking business. Young woman probably

going too fast seemingly went off the road at this bend, through the hedge and into that deep pond behind. She was trapped inside the car and drowned'.

'Drowned?'

'Yep. Happened last Friday. A dog walker found her and called the emergency services but when they arrived and got her out she was a dead-un. Hardly a mark on her I gather apart from a nasty cut to her face but she was dead as a doornail when they pulled her out. Pretty girl apparently. Sad isn't it?'

I was totally shocked. 'Last Friday you say?' I asked weakly feeling my legs go all wobbly. 'She was killed last Friday? Three days ago?'

'Yeah but we've been too busy to get here before today. Police said it wasn't urgent as there was no other vehicle involved and they'd got the body out and as it was obvious what had happened there was no rush. Shame though when a young life is lost. No idea who she was but I expect the police know as they'd trace her from her phone, stuff in her handbag or the car registration I expect.

Hearing the other trucker call him he nodded, gave a thumbs up sign then pressing some controls watched as the car still dripping water was gradually hauled onto the truck. When it had been properly secured the man smiled, said 'Right we're off. Sorry to have held you up mate' and with a cheery smile swung himself into the cab where his colleague had already started the engine. Slowly going backwards and then forwards it did a five point turn in the lane then giving me a wave they drove away leaving me staring at where the car had been and still feeling utterly shocked.

Friday I'd been in Wokingham with Lawrence and Natalie. Alice had died on Friday, but I'd seen her, spoken to her and slept with her yesterday.

That was Sunday.

But how could I have done that? She'd been dead for forty eight hours by then. I shivered as the thought crossed my mind that I'd made love to a ghost. No wonder she'd been so cold and her voice so dull and also no wonder I hadn't been able to find her when I'd been looking for her after I'd woken up.

Alice a ghost? No that was impossible. Completely ridiculous.

This was real life, not television or a Hollywood film. The Alice I'd seen and slept with yesterday was no apparition, no spirit, and no ghost. She'd been there with me in my car, in my cottage and in my bed. She'd been real. Hadn't she?

Shaking my head I turned round and walked slowly and very thoughtfully back to the cottage where as soon as I was inside I poured myself an extremely large whisky which I swallowed in three quick gulps. Pouring another I sat down on the settee, leaned my neck back against the headrest and sipping the second drink more slowly went over in my mind again what had happened yesterday.

But still unable to comprehend what I'd heard from the breakdown truck man, slowly almost as if in a trace, I got up and walked upstairs to the bedroom. I looked at the bed but my eyes immediately focussed onto and stared at one of the two pillows. The one on which she had rested her face when I brought her back yesterday. Two whole days after her death.

Because there clearly to be seen right in the middle

of it like a port wine stain on a white damask tablecloth contrasting against the white linen was a dark red mark. Dried blood from the cut on Alice's dead face.

THE END

The past is a ghost, the future a dream
and all we ever have is now.
Bill Crosby.

I look for ghosts; but none will force
Their way to me. 'Tis falsely said
That there was never intercourse
Between the living and the dead.
William Wordsworth.

> *Evil is just a point of view.*
> **Anne Rice.**

TOM'S OAK

CHAPTER 1

It was a lovely day for a horse ride and Sarah and I were cantering along happily enjoying the sunshine the blue sky and the sheer joy and exhilaration of being out in the countryside riding our horses.

We used to live in Kings Lynn but as we both shared the pleasure and enjoyment of riding we had looked for a nice cottage somewhere out of the town and in the country. Our ideal was a small village, if possible with all the accoutrements that went with it, like a pub, a little shop, a village hall where local events would be held, friendly neighbours, minimal traffic and peace and seclusion.

It took some searching but we found it eventually not far from the market town of Fakenham and fortunately we were able to sell our modern terraced townhouse quickly which was something of a relief as not only had we seen our ideal cottage in our ideal village, but also because of the present state of the property market. We had to drop five thousand on the asking price but the estate agent said that we should do that and snap off the hand of the prospective buyer. So that's what we did. We snapped. We sold. We moved out. We moved in. We loved it.

Now the cottage had been described by the estate agent as *"being in need of some renovation and modernisation".*

I don't think that estate agents are liars, I just think that they see the truth differently from everyone else as in reality it was a shit tip. That was the only way to describe it.

Every room not only needed re-decorating but there was mould and damp to deal with in some of them and upstairs most of the floorboards had to come up and be replaced as they were riddled with woodworm. All of those tasks and more we tackled together, cursing as we found yet more problems and laughing as we solved them. The electrics needed ripping out and completely replacing as did the plumbing. To the side of the house was a brick lean-to but we'd got planning permission from the Planning Authority to incorporate it into the main building, knock through and re-roof it in keeping with the main cottage and that was to become a downstairs loo and shower.

Neither of us were great d-i-y experts but we learnt as we went along and a most helpful man in the superstore in Kings Lynn gave us lots of advice as did various people in the village.

The postman called Harold turned out to be a fund of knowledge as to where skilled craftsmen, as well as labourers could be found and recommended 'Bert, the best brickie for miles around; Jim, bit simple but a hard worker; Stu the sparky, what he doesn't know about electrics isn't worth knowing; Pete the plumber, not the cheapest but does a nice neat job which doesn't leak afterwards'.

The garden was surprisingly large but badly overgrown and to the side of the cottage were some outbuildings from which the roofs had disappeared and one side wall had partly collapsed but we could see that once these were repaired they could become stables, a tack room to keep all the saddles and riding gear and a horse feed storage area.

We worked like Trojans every evening until late and every weekend. We stopped our social life, hardly saw friends, didn't go out for meals, to clubs or the cinema and slowly over the months the cottage took shape and started to become the home that we'd always wanted. It was tough doing it in the evenings after a hard day's work but we'd get home, gobble a quick meal, change into old clothes and get started. We'd taken possession of the cottage in February but the place simply wasn't fit to live in so we'd bought a large mobile home which was delivered and installed and that was where we lived for the next few months.

It was bitterly cold in the mobile home, or "crappy caravan" as we called it, and it was absolutely freezing working in the cottage but we persevered cheered by the thought that we were creating our dream home and at the end of each night we would retreat to the caravan, strip off, take turns in the tiny shower cubicle with its miserable weak shower unit that really only ever produced a trickle of water, get clean of brick dust, plaster, cement, sawdust and all the other detritus that seemed to stick to our hair, body, hands and legs. The cubicle was so tiny that it was only possible to get one person in at a time and so the opportunity for a bit of hanky panky in there under the trickling water was right out of the question, much to the disappointment of us both!

Usually after we'd cleaned up we'd go to bed and drink a mug of hot coffee and a glass of whisky then we'd cuddle, kiss and make love as we found that was the best way to get warm and celebrate the progress that we'd made that night.

Sarah worked just as hard as me and we were both constantly tired, often fed up, always frustrated that progress seemed to be so slow, frequently depressed when we hit a setback, but overall happy that we really were creating our own home just as we wanted it to be.

Once a month though we treated ourselves to an evening off, usually a Saturday and we dressed up, went out to dinner or the cinema, or just out to a pub. Anything to get away from the depressingly constant grind of working on the cottage. These evenings out were like finding an oasis in the desert. Also sometimes on our evening off we met up with friends to whom we'd explained that we were basically going into purdah until we'd finished but that when we had we'd throw an enormous party.

I suppose it was in early August when suddenly we realised that not only was all the construction, re-construction, knocking down and re-building, replacing and renovating work done but as we'd finished decorating and furnishing the kitchen, bathroom and our bedroom then given only a few more weeks work we'd be all finished everywhere inside the cottage at least.

We were able to re-sell the caravan back to the dealer from whom we bought it admittedly for five hundred pounds less than we paid for it but it had served its purpose and was no longer required.

However the garden and outbuildings still had to be tackled but postman Harold recommended 'Old Vera Stone' who lived in the next village. 'Don't ever call her

Vera though always Mrs Stone, but she'll sort out yer garden for yer'.

And she did. In a way I wasn't surprised as if I'd been a weed, bramble or other growing thing that shouldn't be in a garden I'd have given up and died straight away as soon as I saw her.

Harold had said that he'd mention our need to Mrs Stone and she turned up unannounced one Saturday morning. The moment of her arrival was slightly unfortunate as Sarah had been bending forward tugging at a brick which she was trying to dislodge from the middle of the overgrown path and on which she'd tripped and stubbed her toe. Having just come outside and seen her delightful bum in its tight but grubby jeans poking towards me, I'd tip-toed up to her, slid my hands around her waist, leaned forward to kiss her ear and pressing my crotch against her bottom had started to simulate making love to her. She giggled and reacted by pressing herself back against me while twisting her head round to say 'Hey horny man wait till tonight and I'll ....'

I saw her eyes widen as she looked over my shoulder. Quickly she disengaged herself from me stood upright and turned to face whoever or whatever it was that had caught her attention.

'Well really! I must say' said a somewhat stentorian female voice.

I too turned and before us stood a huge woman who was not far off six feet tall and almost as broad but somehow didn't seem fat. Just big. She was holding a bicycle at her side behind which was a long trailer in which could be seen a selection of rakes, hoes, forks and shovels together with an enormous roll of string, shears, clippers, hose reel, buckets, watering can, strimmer and mower as well as a range of smaller gardening implements.

'Err sorry about that' I said standing up and feeling as well as probably looking rather awkward.

'Yes sorry' muttered Sarah. 'We were just fooling around. Can we help you?'

'I am Mrs Stone. I gather from Harold that you require gardening assistance' then she paused and looked around before continuing 'and from the state of this place I should think you do. It is a disgrace. A positive disgrace to allow what could be a beautiful garden to turn into this rubbish tip!'

'Yes' I replied suddenly feeling a mixture of emotions. Embarrassment that she'd caught us doing what we had been; shame at the state of the supposed garden; but also some annoyance that this bloody woman had walked in without being invited and given us a bollocking about the garden. 'We've not lived here long and so far we've concentrated on getting the cottage renovated. We kind of left the garden till later but you're right it is a tip'.

'Well?' she demanded.

'Umm well what?' Sarah asked quietly.

'Well do you want me to sort it out for you?'

'Yes I think so if you would please' I added.

'Good. My rates are five pounds an hour. I never drink coffee, only proper leaf tea not teabags, freshly made and not allowed to stew and I like a digestive biscuit with it. This weekend I'll work here all day today and all tomorrow and then each morning next week until we've got it shipshape. After that probably a morning once a week would keep it in order. You see I can't work here in the afternoons as I help out at the charity shop in Kings Lynn. So shall I make a start?'

'Thank you. Yes if you would. Umm when would you like a cup of tea?' smiled Sarah.

'Well one now to start me off would be nice and then another in a couple of hours. Or if you're ok about it and don't mind I'll just pop into the kitchen and make my own tea when I need it. That'll save you running around after me won't it?'

'Yes that's fine by us. Feel free. I'll show you where everything is' and as Sarah led the large lady indoors I walked over to the tumbled down outbuildings as I'd intended to make a start on them today.

Sarah told me later that Mrs Stone had followed her into the kitchen, pronounced it beautiful, asked to 'Have a little peep around the rest of the place dear?' commented favourably on what we had created, said that she was impressed that we'd done so much of it ourselves and finally when in they were in our bedroom had turned to her and with a grin said 'Good job you had jeans on love wasn't it?'

'Pardon' Sarah had responded.

'When your husband was trying on that bit of nonsense with you in the garden. I mean if you'd been wearing a skirt he'd have hoiked that up, whipped your drawers down and had his way with you wouldn't he?'

Giving a huge laugh she added 'this is such a lovely room you should let him sort you out in here tonight my love, on that' and she'd pointed at our new king sized double bed.

Slightly embarrassed Sarah wasn't sure how to respond but as she struggled with what to say Mrs Stone continued 'Personally I've never really fancied it outdoors. My Herbert used to try it on years ago when we were first married and we often went for walks in the country but I always told him to keep himself under control. I remember one time though he didn't as we were having a bit of a cuddle on the grass and he suddenly dropped his trousers so I pulled up a nettle and pocked his thingy with it. Coo he didn't half yell' she chortled. 'Right my dear I think you're making a lovely home here so now let's get the garden sorted out to compliment it shall we?'

In spite of her bulk she worked hard and notwithstanding her many trips to the kitchen each time emerging with a mug of tea and a biscuit she toiled diligently and by the end of that first day at least half of the garden had been cleared of the overgrowth which she made into a pile at one side and set it alight stoking it at regular intervals so that when she left that night it was possible to see what an impact she'd made.

As we went to bed still revelling in the joys of a bath rather than just the scrappy little shower which the caravan had, Sarah had turned towards me and relayed the conversation with Mrs Stone earlier in the room.

'So are you going to follow her advice?' I queried raising an eyebrow in what I hoped was an interesting and cheeky manner.

'Oh I don't think we should listen to village old wives tales do you?' then she gave a little scream as I said that we certainly should and pulled her on top of me.

'Right now sort me out wench, wasn't that her phrase?' and sliding my hands under her nightie I lifted it up over her buttocks, back and shoulders and dropped it on the floor before gently rolling her onto her back and sliding on top.

Next morning it was Sunday and so I walked to the little village shop to get the papers. Di the shop keeper's wife grinned as I paid. 'You'd better buy some extra tea and digestives as I see you've got Mrs Stone working in your garden' she smiled.

So eventually the rest of the cottage, the garden, the little front driveway which we re-gravelled, the barn and stables, in fact everything was finished and had taken shape.

We were very happy there in our cottage home that we'd created to our own design and requirement. We were also extremely happy with each other and planned to enjoy the cottage, the village and the countryside for at least three years before we started trying for a baby at which time we intended to get married.

CHAPTER 2

Riding was something which we both enjoyed and in fact we'd originally met at a local riding stables just outside Kings Lynn where I'd started to have riding lessons. Sarah had been one of the instructors helping the stable yard owner out at weekends by teaching pupils of the riding stables in return for free board and lodging (known as livery) for her horse.

She told me I was a quick learner but whether that was true or she was just a very good instructor I don't know, but I certainly got great pleasure from it and found riding was not only an ideal way to see more of the countryside but excellent exercise and a real change from my day to day work as Eastern Sales manager for an engineering company. Their head office was in Cambridge which required me to spend large amounts of time behind the wheel of my company car seeing the larger clients in this part of the country, or meeting up with any of the five salesmen that I had reporting to me on "my patch" which covered Norfolk, Suffolk, Lincolnshire and a little bit of the northern part of Cambridgeshire.

Sarah also had a good job as secretary to the Finance Director of a meat processing company in Wisbech.

So our Monday to Friday days were taken with commerce in one way or another but neither of us needed to work at weekends and she, having ridden since she was a child had bought her own horse, now kept it at the livery stables where I met her and I, having decided to start riding fortunately had picked that particular establishment to teach me.

I went on Saturday and Sunday mornings and to

start with I had a rather surly chubby lump of a spotty girl called Tash teach me and although she did get me to understand and then master the basics of riding she always gave an attitude of doing the minimum she could to help me and I found the activity of sitting atop a powerful animal like a horse, both daunting and slightly frightening. Nevertheless I persevered for several weeks but one Saturday when I arrived at ten o'clock for my lesson I was advised by the stable owner that Tash was unwell and someone called Sarah would take her place instead.

When this young woman called Sarah walked briskly to me I was smitten with several things at once. Her attractive appearance, tall, long hair, long legs looking really stunning in her tight jodhpurs unlike Tash's baggy riding trousers, obviously a nice figure but what struck me most was her lovely smile which seemed to light up the whole of the stable yard. It certainly lit me up!

She was so different from Tash in that she really tried to find out what I was finding difficult to properly master and then took time to patiently show me how to overcome the problem. Under her tutorship my riding suddenly came on by leaps and bounds and when we finished the lesson she'd asked me if I wanted to start jumping the next time.

'Well yes alright' I'd replied 'err but only if you'll teach me, not Tash'.

With a twinkle in her eyes she asked 'Alright but you'll have to be a good boy and do everything that I tell you?'

'Ok'.

'Next Saturday morning then? I'll switch lessons around and take you at twelve'.

'No chance of tomorrow is there? I'd like to strike while the iron is hot so to speak'.

'Let me look at the schedule. Sundays are busier as more people come for lessons then and I need to ensure that the jump schooling arena is free'. This conversation had taken place with her looking up at me from the ground and me leaning down from the horse. 'Right you walk Boy Black to his stable, untack him, rub him down, put a rug on his back and ensure he's got some hay to munch while I go and check the schedules'.

'Yes boss' I grinned and for a moment watched her cute bum encased in the tight jods as it moved delightfully to her purposeful stride then as instructed I made the horse walk slowly back from the field in which we'd been working towards the stables, along the concrete yard and arriving outside his particular box halted the animal, dismounted and led him inside the slightly dim interior which strongly exuded horse smells. Just as I'd finished untacking and had thrown a light rug over his back to prevent him catching a chill as he cooled down, Sarah opened the stable door and came in.

'I could do you at eight. I know it's early but I'm booked solid with lessons from nine right through until twelve thirty and then I've got to rush home, bath, change and get to Fakenham as I'm meeting someone for lunch'.

I said it was fine and that I'd happily accept that time.

Next morning I was up very early as I was not only really looking forward to my first jumping lesson but I was keen to see Sarah again and when I arrived at the stable yard at ten to eight she was already there but she had a different horse saddled up and waiting for me.

'Err I usually ride Boy Black' I said.

'Yes I know but although he's gentle when being ridden he's got a mighty big jump in him. In fact he only knows one way to jump and that is to see how near to the sky he can get which might not be ideal for your first lesson' she laughed. 'This is Norfolk Lady and she is kind, gentle, a very careful jumper and will look after you, just like I will' and her smile really was delightful.

She followed on foot as I rode admittedly somewhat nervously out to the jumping area where she'd already laid out some poles on the ground and over the next thirty minutes or so Norfolk Lady and I hopped over them, then as Sarah balanced them on supports so the poles were about a foot off the ground we did little jumps and then she raised them about two feet and we did bigger little jumps and I was getting used to the somewhat odd feeling as the horse lifted off and landed.

To start with I was extremely wobbly but gradually I started to get the feel and hang of it helped by Sarah's kind constant encouragement and advice. In fact I was feeling a bit cocky until as I was riding up the field to one of several slightly bigger jumps that she'd set up, as we approached it the horse sort of veered a bit to the left as she jumped and I was partly unseated when she took off but then completely unseated as she landed. The net result was that I crashed to the ground and lay there winded in breath and embarrassed in spirit.

Sarah ran over to me and knelt down looking anxiously at my face. 'Hey Matt are you alright?'

'Yeah I think so. Everything seems to move. What happened?'

'You fell off' she replied still looking worried.

'I know that but why? I'd been doing so well up to then?'

'Yes but you confused her. She thought you were going for the right hand jump but you suddenly aimed at the left hand one. It is important to ensure a horse knows where it is supposed to go and suddenly surprising it like you did is bound to make it react and with you not yet being very experienced then things like this happen. Now are you sure you're alright?'

'Umm but you said you'd look after me and you didn't'.

'Sorry about that. Now come on I'll give you a hand to get up. Take it slowly though'.

'No wait'.

'What is it, do you hurt?'

'No but will you come out to dinner with me or for a drink maybe, or well anything? Please?'

She looked at me and smiled. 'I guess it's the least I can do for not looking after you isn't it?'

'Yes exactly'.

'All right yes I'd like to. Thank you. Now get up or people will think you are really hurt and my reputation as an instructor will be shot to pieces!'

I stood and gingerly felt myself all over but as I'd discovered while lying on the ground everything worked and it was mainly pride that was damaged.

She suggested that I do one more jump and then finish, so as she held Norfolk Lady I clambered back into the saddle, gathered up the reins, made sure my riding hat was correctly in place on my head and gently kicking the horse into action lined up in front of a little jump, trotted towards it and with my heart in my mouth safely jumped it. Then as suggested I rode back to the stables.

Sarah helped me untack the animal and then agreeing to meet me for a drink on Tuesday evening, smiled and said goodbye.

At the time neither of us was in any form of proper relationship with anyone else. Sarah had an on and off boy friend and I was free and easy with no particular girlfriend although several that I met up with from time to time and a couple of them with whom I slept occasionally.

The Tuesday evening that we met seemed to fly by and at the end we both said we'd enjoyed ourselves and to my great relief she agreed to meet me again on Friday on which occasion we had a meal and as I drove her home to her parents house in Heacham, a small village on the north Norfolk coast we chatted and said we'd like to meet again. After I'd pulled up on the driveway of the house I leant forward to kiss her and to my delight she didn't try to stop me. However it was little more than a peck on the lips but as I tried to make it more passionate she pulled away, took my hand and squeezed it, said thank you for a lovely evening, opened the car door and slid out.

Looking back in before closing the door she flashed that lovely smile as she queried 'You didn't say if or when you'd like to meet again?'

When I replied 'Tomorrow?' she grinned and said yes and to pick her up at eight.

After that we became what is known as an "item" and we found great pleasure in each other's company and it was about six weeks and many dates later that she let me make love to her.

It happened in my little rented studio flat and it was wonderful. I discovered that she wasn't a virgin and obviously nor was I, but we just sort of clicked in bed and the experience was better than it usually is on a first time occasion. In fact it was brilliant and it wasn't just me that thought so. Afterwards when we'd both calmed down and were just cuddling in to each other I asked if it had been alright for her. She grinned as stroking my chest she gave me a little lip peck, said thank you and thought that it had been a Carlsberg experience.

'A what?'

'Matt love, what do Carlsberg say in their advertising?' she asked before kissing me again.

'Something about probably being the best lager in the world?'

'Uh huh, so?'

'Ah so are you saying probably the best lovemaking in the world?'

'Well I've not experienced the *whole* world of course but yes I think I could say it was ...... well you work it out for yourself' and that lovely smile flickered around her face before she kissed me again deeply and passionately.

We dated regularly after that and some eight months later I rented a proper one bedroom flat and Sarah moved in with me. Her parents weren't wholly pleased with this arrangement but they were a charming couple and soon got used to the fact that their only daughter was living in sin.

I continued riding and eventually with Sarah's help not only became quite competent but also bought a horse from a friend of hers as my skill in the saddle had come on so considerably that we both thought I was ready for my own horse.

Soon after that I joined the West Norfolk Foxhounds. Sarah had been a member for years as had her parents who both rode, but for me it was a whole new experience. To my surprise and pleasure the other members of the hunt were friendly to me, didn't criticize or look down on me as I was still a fairly inexperienced rider and indeed they went out of their way to make me feel welcome. I don't think this was just because of Sarah and her long association with the Hunt and its members, many of whom were friends of hers or her parents, but it was just the way they were.

We hunted together regularly on Saturdays during the season and occasionally we'd both take a day's holiday off work mid week to hunt on a Wednesday.

Of course following the passing of the Hunting Act, I gather that the actual hunting nowadays with hounds following a scented trail instead of as it used to be where they hunted out and then chased a real fox, is a mere shadow of what it was then but we loved our days out in all weathers and returned home at the end of the day tired, windblown, often chilled to the bone but happy.

After another year we stopped renting the flat and with the aid of a large mortgage bought our first house which was the little terraced property in Kings Lynn and then two years after living in that and because the countryside, country interests and riding were now such an important part of our leisure time we bought the cottage.

CHAPTER 3

Sarah and I used to ride every weekend and also during the evenings in the late spring, summer and early autumn.

We'd converted the outbuildings into three stables, one for each of our horses and a spare in case of ever need. Also I'd knocked down the old big but tumbledown barn and used the bricks and timbers to make a small much lower barn type store in which we kept our hay, straw and I'd created a small kind of inner room inside in which we kept the horse feed.

Initially we'd kept the bags of horse feed in there too but the mice and rats soon found it and chewed holes in the bags and not only was it unhygienic but also large quantities spilled out and was wasted. So we bought some plastic dustbins and tipped the feed in there but it didn't take long before the bastard rats had gnawed through those as well.

So finally I'd decided to build this brick room within the barn and we kept the feed in there in metal dustbins. That finally defeated the little buggers!

We bought a two horse trailer so we could load the two animals and take them to wherever hunting was taking place, or if not hunting we could tow them to the beach and ride along there enjoying the wide expanse of sand and the ability to gallop along the seashore just like they do in films. Norfolk had plenty of places where that was possible but I guess our favourite location for beach gallops was Holkum. In order to tow the trailer Sarah had given up her beloved Renault Clio and bought a Land Rover Freelander which suited her for normal travel as well as having the ability to lug the trailer and two horses around when needed. I continued to drive my company car which was a dull but efficient Ford Mondeo.

But it was one Wednesday evening in June when I was out riding on my own as Sarah had a heavy summer cold and on her return from work had taken some aspirins and gone to bed. I ambled along enjoying the sights and sounds that I came across. Hares and rabbits in the fields, a little muntjac deer hiding in the undergrowth in the wood that I trotted through, many different sorts of birds singing, chirping, flying in the warm evening sunshine.

I'd emerged from the wood and ahead of me beside the track which I was following was a large oak tree. It was tall but had an odd thing about it in that one large branch about twenty feet off the ground stuck out horizontally and stretched over the track almost like a giant arm pointing at the fields.

Pausing I looked up at the branch and the tree wondering what tales it could tell as it was probably several hundred years old. As I finished staring up into the highest branches and looked down again towards the base of the trunk there stood a man who I'd not noticed before. He was dressed in what I can only describe as a kind of doublet and hose, the sort of outfit you see in pantomimes, films or tv plays about the middle ages.

'Hello' I called cheerily. Super evening'.

'Aye 'tis that' he smiled in reply.

'You off to a party?'

'Nay just wearing best clothes for the event'.

'Some sort of special occasion is it then?'

'Aye you could say that' and he gave a kind of wry

laugh 'after all it's not every day that you're going to die is it?'

'Pardon?'

At that moment my horse Archie wriggled and moved a little so I glanced down momentarily as I gathered the reins in one hand but leant forward to stroke his neck with the other. It was only moments until I'd sorted that out and looked towards the strange man again. But he'd gone. I glanced around but he was nowhere to be seen.

I urged Archie to move forward a couple of steps but wherever I looked there was no sign of him. Shrugging and believing that I'd imagined it I rode on but throughout the duration of the rest of my ride that evening I couldn't get the strange meeting out of my mind.

When I got back home I washed Archie down to get rid of the sweat, then dried him off and gave him a bucket with a small quantity of feed in it for him to munch as I wiped the saddle, reins and bridle down, rubbed them with some special saddle soap, gave them a quick polish and hung them up in the area of the barn where we kept the horse equipment, then leading him out of his stable I walked him to the paddocks and turned him out to graze. Sarah's horse Golden Morn was already in the field and the two animals trotted towards each other, nuzzled and rubbed noses then settled down to munch grass beside each other.

Shutting the gate I walked indoors, went quietly upstairs and peeped into our bedroom and saw that Sarah was fast asleep so being careful not to wake her I collected some non riding clothes, tiptoed out and along the landing to the bathroom where I stripped off and stood under the shower.

When I'd finished I dried myself and dressed in a tee shirt, boxers, pair of jeans and some leather slip-ons crept downstairs where I got a steak out of the fridge and soon had it sizzling on the grill. I chucked some salad in a bowl and sloshed on olive oil and lavender vinegar which we make ourselves from the lavender that grows in the garden steeped in white wine vinegar, some sea salt and ground black pepper. Mixing the salad and dressing together I realised that I'd made far too much as usual but getting a beer out of the fridge I sat by the open kitchen door enjoying the view over the fields as I waited for the steak to finish cooking.

When it was ready I sat outside on the little patio we'd created which ran from the kitchen door along the back of the house past the sitting room french windows watching the sun going down and in the process throwing some wonderfully beautiful golden and red streaks into the clouds.

As I chewed I reflected on two things. Firstly I never managed to get a steak which I cooked as tender as one cooked by Sarah and secondly I thought about the strange man I'd met. Well I mused had I met the man or had I just imagined him?

After considerable thought which also coincided with me finishing my steak and salad I decided that I'd imagined it. I mean after all who would suddenly appear and say that they'd dressed up as they were going to die? No it was utterly mad and I dismissed the whole matter as a figment of my imagination as I walked back indoors, put the dirty plates in the dishwasher then shutting the machine's door I flicked on the kettle and leaned against the kitchen units mulling over yet again what I'd seen and heard.

The kettle boiling brought me out of my reverie and soon I'd put the whole matter out of my mind as I settled down in the sitting room to catch up on the day's paper, drink my coffee and sip a glass of whisky. I watched the ten o'clock tv news, then crept up to bed and after undressing as quietly as I could I slid into bed alongside Sarah who sneezed, muttered 'Hello I feel awful do you want to sleep in the spare room?' and when I said that I didn't she grunted and turned over facing away from me.

I lay tossing and turning partly as a result of Sarah being restless as she snuffled and sniffled but also because every time I closed my eyes I again saw the man at the oak tree. It was a pity that Sarah was feeling so rotten as I'd really have liked to talk to her about it but that wouldn't be fair and so eventually I drifted off to sleep still with the issue unresolved in my mind.

Next morning Sarah was still full of streaming cold so as I left for my day's appointments I agreed to call her boss to say that she just didn't feel up to going into work. When I did so he was fine about it, in fact really nice and understanding and said to tell her to stay in bed and get better soon.

All the rest of that day I kept turning over in my mind the strange encounter the previous evening. The morning was taken up with two appointments with major customers and then after lunch I met up with and spent the rest of the afternoon accompanying one of my sales team to some of his customer visits until around five when we'd finished seeing clients for the day. Then I spent an hour or so in the car with him reviewing progress, agreeing a new set of objectives for the next month and generally giving him what I hoped he'd take as positive and encouraging feedback on his overall performance. He seemed cheerful enough and thanked me for my comments, ideas and suggestions.

I got home about seven and Sarah was up and about but although still looking a bit peaky she not only felt much better than last night but also well enough to have cooked spaghetti bolognese for our supper.

I felt a bit jaded, probably as a result of not sleeping too well last night and also I'd driven a fair few miles today, so I decided not to ride this evening but when we'd nearly finished eating I told Sarah what I had seen, or rather what I thought I'd seen when out riding the previous evening.

'Were you drunk?' she laughed.

'No stone cold sober. I know it's daft but honestly he was standing there and spoke to me, then when I looked again he'd gone'.

'Perhaps you saw a ghost' she suggested then as we'd both now finished eating she stood up, collected the plates and soon returned to the table with a plate of cheese and a bowl of fresh fruit.

'Do you think I did see a ghost?'

'I've no idea. Tell you what though next time we ride out together we'll go past your oak tree and have a good look then maybe I'll see your man as well eh?'

***

I was late home on Friday as the company usually had a meeting at its head office in Cambridge on Friday afternoons which all the four Sales Managers like me attended to discuss problems that we'd encountered, review delivery performance from the factory, customer issues and generally exchange opportunities and problems among ourselves and with Scott Wilson who was the Sales Director of the company and our boss.

He was a good guy and we all liked working for him and although he was tough and constantly pushed for improved results nevertheless he was extremely fair and always available to offer help or advice if needed.

The Friday afternoon meetings started at two o'clock but all of us sales managers used to meet up in a local pub for a sandwich and a small beer beforehand then go to the meeting which generally finished about five thirty although sometimes, like this evening, it had gone on a little longer and so it was almost eight o'clock when I got home.

I didn't mind as they were a good company, paid well, offered the opportunity to earn commission on top of salary and if your team was top team for a two month sales campaign then additional bonuses or prizes could also be won by the sales managers. As there were six campaigns per year and four sales regions then the chances of winning were reasonably high and this year I'd already won a three day holiday in Spain for two; a one hundred pound shopping voucher which Sarah promptly pocketed and soon spent, and an expensive bottle of malt whisky.

I enjoyed working for them and was good at what I did. It meant that I worked long hours but as a result I enjoyed the salary, commission and rewards.

***

So it was Saturday morning when Sarah and I rode out again. Her cold had completely gone and although she had been left with a slight cough nevertheless she was cheerful and completely back to her normal happy self.

The day had started well as after I'd made us each a mug of early morning tea and brought it upstairs, we'd sat in bed talking and sipping then I'd suggested that as the tea was too hot to drink straight away and she was obviously feeling better why didn't we find something to fill in the time until it had cooled down a little.

With a cheeky grin she said that she couldn't think of a thing to do and did I have any suggestions? But the fact that she'd slid her hand down inside my boxers and started to gently rub me down there tended to belie the truth of what she was saying! So when some time later we both sat up again and leaned back against the head board of the bed, the tea was cold!

After breakfast Sarah did a quick tidy round of the cottage while I checked both her and my e-mails but neither of us had anything of importance so we were soon out at the stables, had brushed down the horses, saddled up and set off in the June warm morning sunshine. It was really delightful riding along and once again I was so glad not only that I'd decided to learn to ride but that I'd chosen the particular riding stables that I had but especially that Tash had been ill that morning and Sarah had taken her place.

We'd agreed where we were going to go this morning and had decided on a long ride which would take at least a couple of hours. We rode along tracks, roads, through woods, splashed through a fast flowing but shallow river and eventually came to the side of the wood where what I thought of as "my" oak tree stood.

I could see it in the distance and it was exactly as I remembered it, tall, thick trunk and with that one long sideways branch stretching out across the track. I slowed down as we approached and Sarah adjusted the pace of her horse to match mine.

'Right this is where I saw that chap' I called across to her as I pulled Archie to a halt and I sat looking around as Sarah drew alongside me.

Leaning forward she spoke quietly and encouragingly to her Golden Morn who unusually for him had started to fidget and give a few little bucks. 'Whoa boy, hold still, we'll soon be off again' then looking at me she said 'well there's no one here now except us is there?'

'No'.

'Shall we get on then?'

'Uh huh' and with a last look around I squeezed Archie's flanks and he walked forward. I glanced over my shoulder but there was no-one else there and certainly no sign of my strange man. But there was definitely an odd feeling. Of what I didn't know and couldn't say but there was undeniably a presence of something there.

As we moved off the feeling disappeared and as Sarah followed me her horse calmed down and we were soon cantering along the track until we came to the edge of a huge field in which the corn was already well up and starting to turn from green to yellow indicating that it was early and would soon need harvesting as a result of the long hot dry May and early June after a wet March and April which had got the crop off to a great start and now the heat was bringing it on well.

Like most farmers this one had left a margin at the side of about eight yards uncultivated and it was into this that we turned and kicked our horses into a gallop and immediately they leapt into fast action and we were pounding along side by side. Surprisingly quickly the end of the field started to loom and slowing we came down into a canter and then a trot as we approached the open gateway at the end of the field and soon we were back on a track having enjoyed the exhilaration of a full gallop.

But I was still puzzled by the sensation of something having been there and over the rest of the day from time to time my mind jumped to that old oak tree.

CHAPTER 4

On Sunday Sarah's parents came to lunch. Because it was so hot then rather than serving a full roast she'd cooked a large piece of beef on Saturday evening and we had it cold along with some fresh salmon and a selection of salads, pickles and fresh crusty bread which I'd bought that morning from the village shop where they baked it fresh each day on the premises. Well baking is rather grand description because what they actually did was put some frozen pre-formed dough into an oven and heated it for a while and hey presto out came freshly baked loaves. Still it was a nice and hopefully profitable sideline for them, brought people into the shop and folks like us enjoyed the finished result.

We ate out on the patio and it was a pleasant afternoon although I was constantly expecting the usual question from one or other of Sarah's parents and wasn't surprised when Sarah's mother Margaret leaned forward and smiled at us both as she spoke to her daughter.

'Darling thank you for such a lovely lunch and Matt I must say that the cottage and garden is looking absolutely splendid. I can see you are very happy with each other but what would make me and Henry really happy is to hear that you'd decided to get married'

'Oh Mum' chuckled Sarah. 'We will one day but for now we're just happy being together. Aren't we honey?' and she took my hand, lifted it to her lips and kissed it.

'Oh alright. It's just ......'

'I know Mum' interrupted Sarah.

We drank our coffee, Henry and I had a glass of malt whisky from the bottle that I'd won in a recent company competition and we all relaxed enjoying our drinks, conversation and company.

'Henry?' I asked quietly 'do you believe in ghosts?'

'Ghosts? Good God no. Total rubbish. Stuff of idiots and fools. Alright in books or films but not in real life. No definitely not. Somewhat odd question Matt? Why did you ask?'

'Do you Margaret?'

'No I don't think so. Why?'

'Matt thinks he saw one the other evening' giggled Sarah as she returned to the patio from the kitchen with a fresh pot of coffee.

'You saw a ghost?' queried Henry with a look of complete incredulity on his face.

'Well I don't know' and then I explained what I'd seen.

'Sounds very odd to me' ventured Margaret.

'Yes probably some chap fooling around in the woods. Drunk probably or some sort of a prank or maybe as you said he was actually going to a fancy dress party' stated Henry with some conviction.

'Hmm, I'm just not sure' I responded quietly. 'Still never mind. Let's talk about something else'.

And we did but again I couldn't get the vision of the oddly dressed man out of my mind and even as Sarah and I cuddled together in bed at the end of the day he was still there at the back of my brain but popping to the front every now and then.

***

It was Tuesday evening when Sarah had gone for a "girlie night out" with some of her girl friends so as I was alone I wandered out to the garden and walked around looking at the results that Mrs Stone had created last year which was now really coming to fruition. The various shrubs had taken well and there were masses of flowers. Even the lawn looked reasonable although needing a cut so I got out the mower and was soon trundling up and down behind it when I heard a shout.

Outside the line of shrubs which formed the front fence stood Harold the postman now off duty. Surprising how different he looked out of uniform as this evening he was in a pair of light slacks and a short sleeved rather gaudy coloured green shirt.

'Sorry what did you say?' I asked as I switched off the mower's noisy engine and went closer to him.

'I said old Vera Stone did a good job on your garden didn't she?'

'Yes she did. We're delighted with what she's created and thanks again for recommending her. She just comes in one morning a week now to keep it all under control'.

'Pleasure. Has she eaten you out of biscuits?'

'Yes' I laughed 'and drunk us out of tea'.

'And what about vegetables? Has she started to plant them yet?'

'Yes. Well sort of or to be more accurate her husband seems to be the veg man'.

'Ah old man Herbert? Yes he used to grow vegetables commercially. Had a little place over in the next village but he retired a year or so back but he likes to keep his hand in so he turns up wherever Vera sends him. He'll get you a good crop of veggies alright'.

'Well he said he'd plant up later. At the moment he's been preparing the veg beds, digging in compost and manure. We've got lots of that with the horses here. I gather he'll start planting in the autumn. Potatoes, carrots, swedes and various other things for digging up after the winter. Then he's going to plant salad stuff in the spring. He wants me to get a little greenhouse as he said that some things do better in there. We'll see. So are you out for an evening walk then?'

'Yes I take my little dog Candy out every evening don't I girl?' and he glanced down at the little white West Highland Terrier who looked up at him and wagged her tail. 'It's nice to have a gentle wander around taking my time and not be rushing about delivering the post'.

'Yes I'm sure it is. Well you've got a nice evening for it'.

'We certainly have. Right well we'll be off now'.

'Hey hang on a minute. Look while I've got you to talk to there's something that I want to ask as I guess you know most things around here don't you?'

'Shouldn't be surprised. You'd be amazed what we postmen see, hear and learn. So what is it you want to know?'

'Do you know anything about ghosts or spirits around here?'

'Ghosts and spirits?'

'Yes. Look I know this is going to sound stupid but last week I was out riding and I passed a big old tree and beside it there was this man dressed oddly, well kind of medieval style and, look you'll think I'm stark staring mad but we spoke and then he sort of disappeared'.

'Was it by an oak tree over Thursford way?'

'Yes'.

'Ah that'll be Tom's Oak'.

'Tom's Oak?'

'Yeah it's called Tom's Oak. Years ago, well about two hundred and fifty years ago the local Squire here was a nasty bastard. A real tyrant. He exploited the peasants on his land and imposed all sorts of illegal taxes on them. Anyone who objected got evicted and that meant starvation for them and their family so they just knuckled down and went along with it. They had no choice. But they resented him with a passion and many were on the brink of starvation in any case.

Then one day a man suddenly turned up in these parts. Tom Trevelyan was his name. A Cornishman originally but why he travelled all the way from there to Norfolk no one knows. He was a highwayman and he stopped coaches and robbed them but unusually he didn't keep all that he stole just for himself, but gave away a little of it to the poor so they could buy food or seed to grow crops. A bit like Robin Hood was supposed to have done, stealing from the rich to give to the poor.

Of course it wasn't just out of the goodness of his heart as it provided him with allies and possible alibis if he was caught, but probably more importantly places where he could hide out if the sheriff's men were hunting him.

It seems he was pretty successful and although he operated all over Norfolk he tended to concentrate in this area. I guess that was because there were plenty of dense woods around here then in which he could hide.

Any rate one day near Thursford he robbed a stage coach which was carrying the Squire's wife and daughter. He didn't hurt them but they were very frightened and the Squire vowed to catch Tom once and for all because many of the Squire's friends had complained to him that he ought to do something about this dreadful fellow who was causing such mayhem and fear with his holdups especially as the sheriff and his soldiers didn't seem able to catch him.

So Squire Hobson set a trap and Tom Trevelyan fell right into it. The Squire let it be known that his wife and daughter were going to travel to Norwich to attend a banquet and that they'd be travelling in their finest gowns and taking their jewels with them to wear at the event.

Tom got to hear of this and decided that it was too good an opportunity to miss so he laid in wait for the coach.

When it got close to that oak he leapt out and held it up pointing two pistols at the coachman. He ordered the two women out of the coach and they duly stepped down onto the track covering their faces with veils.

As Tom asked them to hand over their jewellery the older woman flung off her coat, hat and veil to reveal that she wasn't a woman at all but one of the Squire's sons. The other woman also flung away her coat, hat and veil and it was his other younger son. Apparently there was a scuffle and in the process pistols were fired and one of the sons was shot and slightly injured. Tom was also wounded in the knee and as a result he couldn't run away and was captured by the coachman and the uninjured son.

Shortly afterwards and hearing the sounds of pistols being fired Squire Hobson galloped up with some other men as he'd been following the coach some distance behind in order to spring the trap.

Being a magistrate as well as a highly influential

man Hobson had Tom taken back to his manor house and locked him in the cellar and the next morning he convened a court in his living room, invited several local dignitaries, many of whom were his friends, to the proceedings and although Tom defended himself robustly he was inevitably found guilty.

He was sentenced to hang and Squire Hobson told him that he would die that very evening at the place where he had wounded his son. But he was allowed a few hours to prepare himself for his fate and when asked if he had any requests before he was taken to his place of execution Tom asked for a decent set of clothes. It's reputed that he said that if was going to swing he wanted to look smart doing so.

The Squire apparently agreed and being about the same size as Tom provided him with what he'd asked for and then in the late afternoon Tom was put in chains, loaded into a cart and taken to the oak tree where the death penalty was to be enacted. But before they hung him from that long horizontal branch, the Squire agreed to allow him to make a short final speech.

However to the Squire's great surprise and considerable annoyance Tom didn't make a proper speech but instead apparently cursed him and his family for all eternity and then cursed all those that had failed to free him from captivity and threatened that he would return and exact his vengeance on anyone who ever saw him again.

Then they strung the poor fellow up though the Squire insisted that in view of what Tom had said he must be made to suffer for as long as possible and so he was hauled up very very slowly and carefully in order to extract the maximum suffering from a slow and horrendously prolonged strangulation. It's said that it took well over an hour before he finally died and I gather afterwards the body was left hanging there for days until one day it was no longer there. No one really knows who cut him down but it is believed that it was probably the local peasants who took the body away and buried it somewhere, possibly out of remorse that they hadn't managed to free him somehow and prevent his death. But exactly whereabouts he lies isn't known.

They also named the tree Tom's Oak or it's sometimes called Trevelyan's Oak although most people just refer to it as Tom's'.

'Good grief. So do you think that I saw the ghost of Tom Trevelyan then?'

'Could be, but for your sake I hope you didn't'.

'Why?'

'Because it is said that his curse still falls upon anyone who sees him'.

'Don't be ridiculous' I laughed slightly uneasily.

'Oh you shouldn't laugh about things like that' Harold replied with a serious expression. 'I mean there's plenty of evidence for it. The Squire who was a robust hale, hearty and healthy man took ill and died of some mysterious illness within six months of Tom's death. The son, who was shot although only slightly injured, died. The other son who wasn't hurt and was the one along with the footman who'd actually captured Tom was attacked by a wild boar a few months later, seriously gored and killed. The footman got bitten by a hornet and the bite went septic. He died in agony from blood poisoning. The Squire's wife was in their garden when she was bitten by an adder and also died. Furthermore the Squire had a daughter but after her marriage she suffered constant miscarriages and never did manage to bear a live child.

In the field opposite that tree many years ago a farmer died when his carthorse for some inexplicable reason turned and trampled him. And there was the dreadful case of Lady Cavendish. Not far from that oak she was thrown out of her little horse and cart and broke her neck as she fell. Died at the spot where she hit the ground and she was a very experienced horsewoman.

Then there was a very eligible young man named Rowland Walbrook who had heard of the stories, pooh poohed them and to prove it camped under the oak tree one night. He was found next morning with his hair completely white and a gibbering wreck. Never did get right in the head again and remained an idiot for the rest of his life. Other people over the years who've seen Tom have suffered illness, accidents, boils, disasters and all sorts of other nasty things.

So no way should you joke or scoff at Tom Trevelyan' he finished pointing his finger while looking straight at me and I have to admit sending a little shiver down my spine.

'Right I won't. Well I'd better be getting back to the mower I guess, so nice chatting to you and thanks for the information about Tom's oak'.

'Ok but you take care now that you've seen Tom'.

With that warning sounding in my ears it was a very thoughtful me who carried on mowing the lawn and later when Sarah returned I relayed the conversation with Harold to her. To my surprise she took it very seriously and said that she didn't want either of us to ride near that tree again.

So we didn't and in future we always avoided that part of the countryside.

CHAPTER 5

The summer was over and we were well into Autumn and I was out riding alone one evening in late September some months after Sarah and I had mutually decided not to ride near or past Tom Trevelyan's oak tree. The rain which had been falling steadily suddenly became really heavy, the wind got up and thunder and lightning started flashing and booming around. Archie was clearly frightened and although I did what I could to calm him using my voice and gentle pats on his dripping wet neck he remained jittery and every time the thunder crashed he jumped and skittered.

I was a long way from home but there was a short cut I could take compared with the route I had intended to go but the problem was that it took me right past Tom's oak.

As I contemplated whether to go that way or not there was another huge flash and almost immediately a crash of thunder so the centre of the storm was getting closer as the time between flash and bang was now very short. Archie was really quite het up now and so that made up my mind for me. Muttering 'Bugger it, come on let's go that way' I wheeled around and moved up from trotting to a canter.

My horse flinched every time the lightning flashed and he wriggled and jerked when the thunder banged but at least I knew that cantering would speed up the return and going the way I had now decided would definitely get me home quickly. I cut across some fields getting progressively wetter and wetter until in the distance I could see the wood with the track alongside it which would take me home quickest but only by going directly past that oak.

Approaching the tree I had my head down concentrating on the ground ahead to ensure I steered Archie away from any difficult areas underfoot to make certain he didn't trip or stumble and it was only as we got closer that I looked up.

To my horror and amazement there seemingly dangling from the branch was a body. I glanced down at the track and then back up but this time there was nothing there. Breathing a sigh of relief that it was just my imagination that had fired up or it had been a trick of the light, I cantered on towards the tree now desperate to get past it and away. But as I came level to it there standing on the ground was the same apparition of a man that I had seen before but this time he didn't smile and there was a look of sheer malevolence on his face which made me shiver.

I pushed Archie into a canter to get clear of this horrible place as soon as possible and giving a quick glance behind me I saw the man, or apparition if that's what it was, still standing there watching me but with the hairs on the back of my neck standing up and with Archie now cantering along at a good pace fortunately I soon had put Tom and his oak well behind me.

As I reached the village about twenty minutes later and came off soft tracks and field margins and onto tarmac surfaced roads I slowed down from a canter to a trot. Everywhere was still being illuminated by constant flashes of lightning while booms of thunder crashed around us, as horse and I come close to the bend in the road from which a turning led off. This was the lane leading to a small group of cottages including ours which was right at the end. Glad that I was nearly home I turned the bend and then swung left into the lane but as I trotted along I could see a group of several people standing around outside our cottage.

A police car was also parked there with its blue light flashing adding to the effects from the lightning. Clearly something was wrong and as I approached the half a dozen or so people standing there parted to let me ride through.

'What's happened' I yelled.

'Lightning struck your cottage' Gerry who lives next door yelled back. 'We heard the huge bang, ran out and saw what had happened. We called the police who've just got here and the fire brigade are on their way'.

I slid off Archie, threw the reins to Gerry's wife Anne and ran towards our cottage. Our lovely cottage home seemed to have collapsed at one end with the end wall, and part of the roof crumpled into a pile of rubble. I ran forward and pushed open the front door, turned right and was met by a pile of debris and the air was full of choking dust. A police officer was there kneeling beside something. He heard me and turned towards me.

'Sir get out the building isn't safe'.

'It's my home. My cottage. Where is my wife? Is she ok?'

'Was she in the cottage sir?'

'Yes I've been out riding. Her horse is lame so she didn't come with me but never mind about that where is Sarah? Where is my wife?'

'Sir there is a woman here on the floor partly buried under the rubble. It looks as though the chimney came down from the roof and through the ceiling and it appears to have landed on her. I am sorry, very sorry to have to tell you sir that she is dead'.

'Sarah dead? No there must be a mistake. She can't be dead?' and I pushed past the policeman to where Sarah's head and one arm could be seen. Kneeling down I felt for a pulse but there was nothing. The police officer was right. Sarah had died in the collapse.

'There must be something that we can do. Look come on let's get her out' I yelled as I started to tear at the brick and rubble with my bare hands to free her. But there was a heavy beam resting across her as well as what was obviously a major part of the brick chimney. I started to cry as I held the hand that projected and muttered 'Sarah my darling'.

Soon a doctor and then the fire brigade arrived but although the fire fighters using lifting equipment managed to move the chimney, the beam and other large pieces of debris the doctor confirmed Sarah had died instantly from the collapse and that sadly there was nothing more that could be done for her.

Gerry and Anne offered to put me up for the night which I accepted but when I did go up to bed there I couldn't sleep and just tossed and turned sobbing for the loss of my beloved Sarah.

Then I remembered what Harold the postman had said about ill befalling people who'd seen the highwayman's ghost and several times in my mind's eye I could again see Tom Trevelyan's face.

I saw him apparently cheerful when I'd first met him months ago however I could also still see the awful impression this evening of that body hanging from the branch. But the overriding and lasting memory which I doubted would ever disappear from my mind was the sheer expression of evil on his face as he stood watching me gallop past his tree tonight.

'Tom Trevelyan, you dreadful, evil, wicked, malicious, hateful bastard' I whispered into the darkness and as I started to cry I wondered if the sound of laughter that I thought I heard was real - or was it just a figment in my mind?

THE END

All evils are equal when they are extreme.
Pierre Corneille.

It is a sin to believe evil of others,
but it is seldom a mistake.
H. L. Mencken.

All that spirits desire, spirits attain.
Kahill Gibran

The ghosts you chase you never catch.
John Malkovitch.

THE COLLEGE

CHAPTER 1

The management college was situated in Norfolk in a village not far from and a little to the south of Norwich. I drove there on the Sunday afternoon as we were expected to check in for the course any time after two o'clock but before five. It was around a quarter past four when I parked in the large car park and heaved my suitcase, laptop and brief case out of the boot of the car. I "blipped" the car locked as I crunched my way across the gravel driveway to the imposing front entrance of the old building.

Inside, a somewhat over officious and rather ugly woman was sitting at a desk. Looking up she stared at me without expression but said 'Can I help you?' with an attitude that indicated that she'd rather be anywhere than here checking in attendees to the college on a Sunday afternoon.

'Hello I'm Greg Thorbone' I smiled 'here for the four week Transition to Senior Management course'.

Tapping the keys of her computer she peered at the screen, sniffed and said 'Ah yes I've got you. Right you're in room two oh nine which is on the second floor of this, the old building I'm afraid. Most of the others on your course are accommodated in the new block but those rooms over there are all taken by people who arrived earlier'.

She said it in a manner which indicated that I was late and that it was therefore my fault that I was in the old building and not in the new wing.

'No problem' I said cheerfully 'I'm sure all your rooms are comfortable whether they're in the new block or this building'.

It was a slightly strange look she gave me as she said 'They're comfortable but those in the new wing are larger. Still you're not over there are you?'

'No. So can you direct me please?'

'Stairs are across the hallway to the right. Second floor. No lift here'.

'I bet there's a lift in the new block though?' I teased.

'Yes there is' she muttered avoiding any possibility of humour 'as well as coffee machines and ice makers. Right you need to assemble in the library at five thirty for introductions and briefing about the course. Any questions?'

'No thanks very much, you've been most helpful'.

Ignoring my sarcasm she said 'Good. Yes can I help you?' and I saw that she'd looked over my shoulder to someone else that I hadn't heard come in. Turning I saw a pretty young woman probably around my own age of thirty who was obviously also about to check in.

I picked up my bags, nodded and smiled at the new arrival and made my way across the impressive hallway to the huge curving staircase that led upwards in an arc to the first floor. As I reached that, I looked down for another glance at the young woman and then turned away and started to climb the second flight of stairs which although narrower was equally impressive. At the top I followed the signs to my room, found the door already slightly open with the key in the door, so I pushed it open wide, dropped my bags to the side of the room and with a gentle kick shoved the door closed.

Checking my watch I saw that I had plenty of time until the five thirty meet up with the other course attendees so I unpacked and stowed my things away. After all I was going to be here for a month so I needed to keep the room which was adequate in size but as the receptionist had indicated not overly large, tidy.

There was a single bed with a bedside table one side built into the headboard, a desk and upright chair, one small armchair, a combined tv, radio and dvd player and peering through a sliding door I found my bathroom which comprised a short bath with a shower unit over, wash basin and loo. It was a room that was adequate and fit for purpose but definitely not luxurious.

I sat down on the bed and bumped up and down a couple of times. Felt ok if a bit on the hard side but at least it didn't creak not that that mattered as I knew from attending a couple of other management courses in the past there wouldn't be a lot of time in bed as we'd be working from early in the morning until very late at night and so bed when I eventually got to it last thing would be solely for the purpose of sleeping. Mind you those earlier courses had each been much shorter and not a whole sodding month.

As I lay down and stared at the ceiling I counted the cracks of which there were four, all of varying length and shape and I wondered how many times I'd stare at them over the next twenty eight days. Sometimes for inspiration, sometimes in despair, sometimes in frustration, sometimes in anger, but for whatever reason those cracks and indeed every single notch, mark and indentation would be studied by me while I was here because when you are incarcerated in a management college like this for four long weeks and you retreat to your room to study alone, to think deeply about a problem that has been set, or just for some peace and quiet then there is very little to brighten your day except staring at the ceiling!

It is always a strange atmosphere at these sorts of places due in part to the wide diversity of people with their various skills, levels of experience, different courses that they were attending, how long they'd been there and how well or otherwise they were doing.

Oddly there is no pass or fail on the type of courses run by this sort of management college. You don't take an exam at the end. They also say there is no feedback to your employer on how well or badly you have done, although I have always harboured a secret doubt about that.

The point is that you are there to learn. Your employer has paid, often extremely large sums of money, to send you there and generally it is those on the management fast track or those for whom the employer sees a bright future that are sent. This is my third such course. The first about four years ago which lasted for five days was about *Managing People* and I was sent when I had received my first proper promotion and was about to start my first management job managing other people. The second was last year and it was a four day *Finance for Non-Finance Managers*, which was hard work but really helped me understand about balance sheets, cash flow, profit and loss and how the financing of a business worked.

But this was the first long course that I'd been sent on and I have to say that I was looking forward to it because in two months time I was to take up my new role in the Company as Commercial Director responsible for the sales, marketing and administration functions of the business.

I'd worked my way up the business having left university with a degree in business studies and had risen up the marketing function as a Brand Manager then a Product Group Manager before being appointed as Marketing Manager which meant that I was head of marketing for the company. In between each of those appointments I had carried out various roles in the Sales operation and so now I was competent and fully familiar with all the elements of sales and marketing. Running the admin side of the company I imagined would be a straight forward and largely common sense activity.

But an opportunity had arisen for promotion into a different division of the company which had been advertised internally, as well as externally, for the post of Commercial Director. I knew I was well qualified and capable of doing it and after several interviews had finally succeeded in gaining the appointment.

However the company had suggested, well insisted really, that I attend an external course of the type that I was here to do before starting the new job. It was sound thinking and I was grateful for the opportunity that had been handed to me and I fully intended to make the most of it, learn as much as I could and whether there was any feedback or not I was determined to ensure that I was the shining star of the group.

So as there was still a little while before I needed to

go downstairs to the library I got off the bed and picked up the folder of information on the desk unit set in front of the window.

There was what was titled a Course Folder which was empty except for a few blank sheets of paper. Next to it was another folder marked "Fire and Safety Rules" and next to it a small booklet with a coloured picture of the old building on the front with the title **WINDSOR MANAGEMENT COLLEGE** embossed in gold on the outside.

I picked it up and dropped down into the upright chair set in front of the desk. Opening the booklet the first few pages were taken with photographs of the various lecture and conference rooms, pictures of the dining room and what looked like a very impressive library. Next came pictures of the grounds and details of the sports facilities available which included an apparently well equipped gymnasium, squash and tennis courts, a five hole golf course with a separate putting green and joy of joys a swimming pool. The final section which ran to several pages was the history of the place.

Originally it was built in the mid seventeen hundreds as a private house for a titled man named Sir Henry Douglas Stevens who'd named it Woodpecker Hall because it was said that having bought the land when deciding exactly where to build his house he'd been walking through a small wood and seen a woodpecker tapping away at a tree obviously creating a home for itself. He saw this as a good omen and hence named it after the bird.

Henry Stevens had made his fortune trading in foreign lands but unlike many others ruined by the South Sea Bubble in the year seventeen twenty he wasn't, although whether that was due to his personal foresight and careful planning which is what he claimed, or sheer luck which was probably more likely no-one was ever sure. But the fact remained that not only did he not get ruined but his already not inconsiderable fortune was soon enlarged as he bought out the worthless assets of many who had been less fortunate and as time improved he sold them at vast profits which he ploughed back into his own business empire which stretched across the globe.

In fact in a way his was one of the first global multinational companies. But Henry was a secretive man who didn't flaunt his wealth, lived frugally and being a devout and God fearing person attended church twice on Sundays with his family where they had their own pew with a brass name plate denoting that it was theirs.

Indeed his one and only real extravagance was in building Woodpecker Hall but even doing that he was creating something of value which would appreciate and become worth considerably more in the future and thus benefit his descendants and heirs.

But time went by and as has happened so often with similar wealthy families when he died his son Archibald inherited the business and the estate. Initially he continued the good work that his father had instigated with such success but eventually he tired of being parsimonious and constantly not spending money on personal pleasures.

His wife who was unable to have children though became concerned because he started gambling in London but unknown to her he also started paying for expensive mistresses of which he set up at least two in their own houses in the capital. Furthermore whenever his wife took herself off for a few days to stay with friends elsewhere in the country then Archibald brought a succession of women into Woodpecker Hall. It was a known scandal at the time but he was so wealthy that no-one on or near the estate dared to say anything and his friends, generally a fickle lot weren't interested in his sanctity as they enjoyed the orgies that he regularly held there. He also succumbed to the clutches and eventual horrors of opium as well as becoming addicted to gin.

In the space of just four short years he'd spent all the money that the business and estate had produced over the years, borrowed heavily, lost all his so called friends and was faced with his creditors demanding repayment.

Whether it was suicide because he was broke, or an accident because he was under the influence of drink, opium or both, was never known but one night his wife having finally departed some days beforehand for a smaller house that they also owned at Cromer on the coast, Woodpecker Hall caught fire as a result of which Archibald was burnt to death and almost three quarters of the house was destroyed. It was rumoured that as well as himself he had some women in the house that also perished in the fire at the same time as did he.

Over the following years it remained a ruin, unlived in and gradually continuing to deteriorate further until eventually it got into such a bad state that no-one seemed to want to buy it as it required completely rebuilding from top to bottom at a vast cost.

Furthermore rumours started that the ghost of Archibald and some women could be seen stalking the ruins at night or sometimes the legends grew that sounds of men and women giggling was heard. Alternatively some people said they could distinctly hear shouting and screaming about the fire. Whatever was or was not heard nevertheless the story stuck and ruined Woodpecker Hall became known as being haunted.

So for many years it remained as a sad destroyed wreck until one day a young man named Reginald, the son of a cousin of the original Henry, having made money from both the slave trade and piracy came ashore and bought it.

It took ten years to rebuild and recreate a faithful replica of the original building and so it remained in Reginald's family for more than the next hundred years until a descendant called George, deciding that the new world of America offered a real opportunity for him and his family, embarked on a small ship to sail across the Atlantic. But the ship foundered in a storm and the entire family were lost. George, his wife Mary and their four children were all gone and as there was no-one to inherit or take over the house once again it fell into disuse.

Over the years it was bought and sold several times but each new owner although initially filled with enthusiasm to renovate and restore the building found one reason or another not to finish the renovation and restoration. Some said it was the crippling expense of restoration. Others blamed ghostly goings on for their inability to complete the work. But whatever the reason Woodpecker Hall continued to fall into further disrepair.

Eventually in the late eighteen hundreds it was bought by a slightly eccentric elderly man called Edward Thornley who devoted a high proportion of his considerable fortune to rebuilding with a view to eventually restoring the house, its grounds and gardens to their former glory.

It took seven years but when complete Woodpecker

Hall was once again the proud beautiful imposing building that it had originally been. Edward threw a huge party and masked ball to celebrate its reopening and over a hundred people attended and afterwards everyone commented on what a splendid evening it had been, however some also observed that they thought that there was a strange atmosphere about the building, especially on the upper floors.

From then on the ownership of the Hall passed down through the ages to various people but the cost of maintaining its fabric and construction rose inexorably and eventually the family then owning it decided enough was enough and simply moved elsewhere leaving the once proud building to yet again gradually start to decay and deteriorate until finally part of one end wall collapsed.

The old house remained unloved and unlived in until a charitable trust bought it as a retreat for those wanting to escape the rigours of everyday life. The members of the trust worked hard themselves and with skilled professional help repairing, rebuilding, renovating and recreating until not only was Woodpecker Hall saved but back into use once again.

The legend of the ghosts of Archibald and the women though continued to thrive and several people reported seeing or hearing them in different parts of the old building but especially on the second floor where it was believed that the fire had started all those years ago. However there were also many reports of the presence of a man but not women in one small room off the big hallway to the side of the main house and those who reported seeing him also commented that his occasional appearances were often accompanied by the smell of burning. In fact some said that they sometimes sensed a presence although they saw nothing, yet they were still conscious of the burning smell.

Eventually in the nineteen seventies the Hall was sold by the Trust to Windsor Management College which had originally been established in the town of the same name to the west of London but as its success in attracting more and more businessmen and women to the courses and development programmes that it offered had flourished so strongly it needed new and larger premises.

The Hall and its extensive grounds appeared a perfect fit for their need and knowing that location wasn't too important as people attending these sorts of programmes were business people and would travel more or less anywhere, the College management felt that Norfolk not only wasn't a handicap, but indeed a possible benefit being very rural, not too difficult to get to and offering many advantages in terms of facilities nearby with the coast, the famous Norfolk Broads and acres and acres of beautiful countryside.

The move was an immediate success and with these larger premises the College was able to offer more courses, more programmes and serve many more people.

By nineteen eighty they were bursting at the seams and after a long fight with the planning authorities they succeeded in getting permission to build a two storey separate addition to the side of but behind the main Hall. It was not attempted to build something in the style of the Hall and so a purpose built block such as is seen at schools, universities and many other institutions was constructed. Screened by trees with a tarmac track way leading through them to reach the new construction, it was ugly, but functional and provided exactly what the College wanted. More bedrooms, more class and lecture rooms, several small syndicate rooms and two large meeting rooms.

The whole thing became a self fulfilling exercise. The additional facilities enabled the College to increase even further its offerings and seeing how successful it was becoming, the planning authorities were reasonably relaxed about future developments and provided that nothing was done to alter, damage or add to the original Hall they were agreeable to some additional development work on the new block and so eventually a third floor was added on top of the two storey building and additional ground floor rooms were also built on.

That was the end of the history the place and so having now finished reading the entire booklet and checking my watch I saw that the time now was ten minutes past five and so I heaved myself off the bed to go back downstairs to have a wander around and familiarise myself with the building, it's facilities and especially to locate two of the college's most important amenities. The bar and the dining room.

Leaving my room I slowly descended the stairs taking time to look at the wonderfully large paintings that adorned the walls on each side of the staircase and as expected they were of men and women from an earlier age. No doubt former owners or relatives of the many past owners of the building which even though now a management college still remained one of the finest houses in Norfolk.

I soon found both the dining room which was of course empty at that time and the room in which the bar was located. This wasn't empty as although the bar itself was unmanned and closed off with a shutter some small groups of people were working in the corners of the room which smelt beery.

Generally there were plenty of other people about so I started to mingle. I introduced myself but none of them were on the course that I was here to attend and so I continued to explore the extensive ground floor of the Hall finding several rooms comfortably furnished with deep armchairs, settees, small writing tables in the corners, coffee tables bulging with newspapers which were in a bit of a mess as they always are after they've been read and put back. Somehow they never close up as tightly or neatly as before they've been read.

It was as I was going from one large comfortable room to another that through a side door came the young lady that I'd seen checking in after me.

'Hello' she smiled 'I believe we're the only ones from our course that old hag put in this building. The rest are in some new block somewhere. I'm Belinda Winkfield by the way' she added holding out her hand. I shook it noting its firm grip.

'Pleased to met you. Greg Thorbone' and as I smiled back I was taken with her pretty dark brown eyes which were carefully but not overly made up, her very kissable mouth, her dark hair which when I'd seen her before was tied in a pony tail but now hung neatly down to her shoulders but what especially held my attention was the openness of the smile on her extremely attractive face.

'Been on one of these sorts of things before?'

'Well I've done some shorter ones but nothing that locks me away in the wilds of Norfolk, and never for a month' she chuckled. 'Still I imagine we'll survive won't we? And what about you? Have you been on management courses before?'

'Yes like you short ones. I did a finance course for almost a week and a five day kind of initial introduction to management course. Also the odd one or two day sessions but like you, nothing of this length. Still as you say no doubt we'll survive. Have you found where we can get some coffee by any chance?'

'Yes in the room next to the library there are several tea and coffee machines and some fridges with a selection of canned drinks, water and snacks. Crisps, nuts, chocolate bars and so on'.

'Next to the library you say?'

'Yes I'll show you shall I as I fancy a coffee myself?'

So we went off together and soon were sipping cups of surprisingly decent coffee as we chatted a little about ourselves and speculated about the course. There were a few other people in the room and over the next twenty minutes or so more people came in and slowly we drifted together in little groups of two, three or four as we introduced ourselves and made small talk.

It was just before five thirty that two people exuding an air of authority strode into the room had a look around, were obviously subtly counting us and then they walked out and made their way into the library shortly followed by all of us.

The library was a splendid room. Tall with every wall lined from floor to ceiling with books of all types many behind protective grills but others available for anyone to take and read. There was a huge selection ranging from novels, thrillers, documentaries, biographies, travel books, atlases, the complete works of Shakespeare, and poetry by famous and unknown poets. One wall was completely taken with books about business and management, while another section had an extensive selection of religious books including tomes on Zen Buddhism; the Vedas which I discovered from a quick peek inside was the book for Hindus; the Guru Grantha Sahib being the primary life and teachings for Sikhism; as well of course as the Bible and the Koran.

In fact around the walls in this library was a book on just about anything that you could imagine you might want to read.

'Right everyone find somewhere to sit and let's all get to know each other a little' beamed one of the two people who'd sized us up in the coffee room.

At one end of the library a selection of upright chairs had been ranged in theatre style and so we all made our way there and picked a chair. I was pleased that Belinda said quietly 'Do you mind if I sit next to you. You are at least one person I know a little' and she smiled that lovely smile again as she settled herself down.

Taking his place in the middle of the room in front of the semi circle of us the man spoke again.

'Hello and welcome. I'm Tony Anderson and this' he nodded to the lady standing a little to the side and away from him 'is Janet Harvey and we are your tutors, mentors, guides, helpers, tormentors and generally the people who will try and keep the course, and you, on a straight and narrow path of enlightenment for the next four weeks'.

He paused and theatrically clapped his hands to his head. 'God four weeks' he exclaimed. 'I don't know whether that's worse for you or us? Us probably!' and we all dutifully laughed as we were obviously supposed to do.

'Ok now look. We are here to help you and if you have any problems, worries, difficulties or issues just come and talk to us. Think of us as your personal problem solvers, as well as your teachers and lecturers because as well as being your personal agony aunt, well uncle in my case, we will be running this course for you. I am the course director and Janet is assistant director' there was a pause as he turned to her and stepped aside.

'Yes hello and let me add my welcome to you all' she said as she took Tony's place. 'We are also here to ensure that you work hard, and believe me you will, and to be certain that the considerable sums of money that your companies have paid to send you here and learn what we have to offer are well spent. So for the next four weeks the key is to forget *everything* and *anything* outside this college.

Forget about seeing husbands, wives, girlfriends, boyfriends. Forget your hobbies, and other outside interests. Forget your career hopes and aspirations. Just spend your time concentrating on what you will learn here from Tony and me, from the other lecturers, from your peer group, from the business documents and papers that you'll read, the books that you'll study and the work that you'll do. I can promise you that we will work you hard and push you more extensively than you have ever been pushed on a course before'.

She paused somewhat dramatically as her words rung around the room then with a small shrug she smiled as she relinquished her position to Tony.

'So have we frightened you? Anyone want to run off now and not stay? No? Good' and he grinned. 'I can also promise you that hard though it will be, it will be fun, well at least parts of it will but that at the end you will have the treasured certificate noting that you've attended the Windsor Management College Transition to Senior Management course and that I assure you will stand you in very good stead for the future in your various careers.

Now some issues of housekeeping' and he then proceeded to cover matters such as fire escapes, meal times, location of nearest chemists in case of need, an outline of the programme, issued us each with a name badge, another course folder and several lined A4 sized notepads.

'Good' said Janet taking up the lead again. 'I think that now would be a good time for us all to get to know each other a little and the best way that do that is if we each in turn stand up and speak about ourselves for two minutes to tell everyone else about you, your company, your job title and what you actually do as titles can be misleading' she smiled 'as well as any hobbies or interests that you have. But most importantly what you hope and expect to get out of this course'. With a look at her colleague she added 'Maybe you'd like to start us off Tony?'

'Certainly' and he then proceeded to explain that he'd retired early from industry a few years ago aged fifty five as he wanted to devote his time to teaching up and coming younger business people all the things that he'd learnt in his long management career and that his particular speciality was motivation of disenchanted individuals. He spoke interestingly and clearly, concluding with the fact that he was married and had been for thirty years, had three children and five grandchildren and that his main interest outside work was restoring an old Jaguar car which he'd bought some years ago as a rusty wreck having discovered it in a barn.

Janet then took up the story about herself and we learnt that she was married with one grown up son, had been a lecturer for many years, specialised in building effective business teams and had been with the college for six years. Her outside work interest she stated as the history of Ancient Greece and whenever she had time she liked to go to that country to study and learn more about it.

Then it was our turn to stand up and say our piece. Belinda and I were about half way through the group of twelve people and she was asked to speak immediately before me and I soon learnt that she was single, lived in Bath, worked in Bristol for an engineering company, was shortly to take up the post of Head of Projects, was ambitious, looking forward to learning lots of new things on this course and that her interests were swimming, tennis and running and when not being sporty then clubbing and having a good time. She spoke well, amusingly and with confidence.

When it was my turn I was pleased that I didn't feel nervous standing up and speaking about myself in front of a group of strangers. I did it ok and finished by saying that although I was looking forward to my forthcoming promotion I was conscious that I still had much to learn in the skills and art of managing people and wanted all the help that this course would give. I noted that both Tony and Janet nodded approvingly while Belinda leaned close to me as I sat down and whispered 'Creep' but she smiled nicely as she did so.

After everyone had finished their two minute self commentary we all knew a little about each other although as one guy had spoken for nearly five minutes we knew a lot more about him. Stupid sod I thought as he droned on and on as the brief had been clear. Two minutes not five. Hopefully I wouldn't get lumbered with him in any syndicate work that we'd be doing as my experience of previous courses was that although quite a lot of the time would be in the main lecture room as an entire group probably fifty percent of our time would be working in small syndicates and I speculated as to whether they'd have us in little groups of three or four?

I later found out the answer was four so there would be three syndicates and during the next four weeks not only would each of us be striving individually to do our best, we'd also be pitching our syndicate activities against those of the others.

'Right' said Tony as lifting a box onto a table at the front of the room he pulled out some bottles of champagne. 'At the end of each week we'll announce which syndicate in our opinion has done best for that week and a celebratory bottle of bubbly will be presented to it. So there are four bottles to be won during the course. In addition at the end of the course we like to give individual prizes to those candidates who we think have performed best on the course as a whole.

We don't refer to winners or losers as there is no real competition and no exam to pass or fail at the end. You are purely here to learn but for the person who at the end of the four weeks we select as having shown either the greatest initiative, improvement, or other outstanding results there is a prize of a weekend for two in London with a show and meals all thrown in. The person who comes next will win a meal for two at a restaurant of their choice and for the third person four bottles of wine. One red, one white, one rose and one bubbly.

So there you are everyone. Good luck and remember *we* are here to help but *you* are here to learn and so *together* we're going to have a great month'.

'We certainly are' smiled Janet then looking at her watch she added 'and I think that the bar should be open by now, so as a welcome tonight your drinks before dinner and wine at the table are on the college. After that all future drinks from the bar or wine at the table, are charged to your rooms and must be settled by you on departure'.

There was a shuffling of chairs and soon we twelve candidates followed Janet out of the room to the bar where we formed little groups and started chatting amongst ourselves.

As is usually the case on this type of course we were quite a mixed bunch. About half including Belinda were around my own age but there were three men who were considerably older, two women also older than me and one chap who looked about twenty five and I wondered why he was here learning about Senior Management as I doubted that he'd even started on junior management yet. But during the evening I discovered that he worked for his father in a family carpet making business and as such was about to join the Board of Directors but before he did so then his father had insisted that he attend this course.

I have always been a good mixer so I didn't find it difficult to wander from one little group to another little group, introduce myself find out a bit about the other candidates and generally settle myself in. After all if we were to be incarcerated together for a month then I thought that I ought to start getting to know my fellow sufferers.

A gong sounded indicating that dinner was ready and we all trooped off to the wooden panelled dining room which would have been quite a dull and dreary room had it not been for the three gloriously large chandeliers which hung majestically down the centre of the room and the matching wall lights all of which actually made it a bright warm welcoming room enhanced by the large open blazing fire full of logs burning brightly at one end of the long room.

The room filled up surprisingly quickly and I suppose that the gong sounding to announce that dinner was ready was a moment of cheer in the somewhat austere, gloomy and hard working academic environment which we had just entered but in which some other residents had obviously been for some days or weeks. There were several tables but we were guided by Janet to one longish table and so we sat six down each side with Tony at one end and Janet at the other. To my disappointment Belinda was right down at the far end of the table on the opposite side.

Two middle aged waitresses offered us a choice of carrot and coriander soup or parma ham and melon to start with and then our main course was a choice of roast beef, roast pork, grilled halibut or cold ham and salad. I had the pork and it was delicious and from the comments of others who had different items everyone noted that the food was good which was important as there would be nothing worse than being here for so long with crap food to eat. Dessert was a choice of trifle, cheesecakes, a sticky chocolate concoction, fresh fruit or cheese and biscuits.

Red and white wine was freely available as was a choice of still or sparkling water. Afterwards we all adjourned to the bar and spent a pleasant enough evening chatting, sipping more alcohol until around eleven o'clock there were only three of us left from our course. Belinda, me and an older chap named Richard.

Finally refusing another drink I said I was off to bed but Richard thought he'd have another nightcap before turning in. As I left Belinda said she was going too and so we walked together out of the bar made our way into the hallway and climbed together up the long winding staircases to the second floor which although adequately lit nevertheless still seemed somewhat gloomy. I stopped outside my room and said goodnight.

She responded 'Sleep well and see you in the morning' and as she continued on along the corridor she called out over her shoulder 'hey it's a bit spooky up here at night isn't it'.

'Yes definitely' I muttered as I watched her back view walking away from me until she was lost to my sight as she rounded a bend at the far end of the passageway. I have to say that I thought she was right as it did seem a bit spooky but that was probably because it was night time and there was no natural light into the corridor from the windows, just the wall lights.

But shutting my door and putting such thoughts out of my mind I had soon peed, washed, undressed and slid into the single bed which although as I'd discovered earlier was a bit on the hard side seemed generally to be comfortable enough. I snuggled down and thought about my fellow course members but especially about Belinda and the delightful vision of her bum moving seductively as she'd walked away from me. It had been a cheerful sight in the gloomy dark corridor. Smiling at the memory I turned onto my side and it wasn't long before I dropped off to sleep.

I woke a couple of times in the night which is unusual for me as normally I sleep like a log and once my head hits the pillow I'm dead to the world until the alarm shatters me awake next morning.

The first time I thought I heard someone whispering but then decided that it was just the wind whistling around the old building rattling the sash windows, but the second time it seemed as though there was someone in the room. Wondering if it was Belinda who'd come to ravish me as I slept, I flicked on the bedside light but there was no-one there of course except me although the wind was obviously still playing strange tricks because when I turned out the light and laid down again I could have almost sworn that I heard footsteps going past my bed.

CHAPTER 2

Next morning dawned bright although still breezy. I woke reasonably refreshed, switched on the room kettle, showered and shaved and then while I dressed I drank the cup of tea that I'd made.

Trotting downstairs I wandered through some of the rooms and discovered that there were already several people about. Some were sitting in easy chairs reading newspapers or books, some obviously here from the previous week or weeks were sitting studying folders of papers, or tapping away at laptops. Others were chatting in two's or threes but what drew me was the delicious smell of bacon wafting throughout these downstairs rooms and so following my nose to the dining room where we'd eaten last night there were many more people in there.

Along one side was a long table laden with dishes which on closer inspection provided to be all the ingredients of a full English cooked breakfast but there were also dishes of fruit of many different sorts, packs of cereals, even a tureen of porridge.

Unlike last night there was no-one serving. It was a self service arrangement for breakfast and so I helped myself to a dish of grapefruit and orange segments, poured a cup of coffee from the glass coffeemaker, popped some slices of bread in the toaster machine and wandered over to a table where I left my fruit and coffee then went back to wait for the toast to cook. When it had I again approached the long table and put some rashers of bacon, a sausage, a tomato, a spoonful of baked beans and one poached egg on my plate and was soon seated again happily munching away and exchanging small talk with some others sitting near me.

Our sessions started at eight thirty and just as I was getting up to wander into the library to find a newspaper Belinda walked in to the dining room. We nodded and smiled at each other and then I found a copy of the Daily Mail and settled down to catch up on that paper's approach to the day's news before we got stuck into our first class,

My folder had indicated that the main lecture room for our particular course was to be one known as Apple and I later discovered that all the different lecture, class and syndicate rooms were named after trees found within the grounds of Woodpecker Hall, although it was no longer known by that name but as Windsor Management College.

At around eight twenty I put the newspaper back on the coffee table and walked out into the hallway, checked the indicator board and then followed the signs to Apple. It was in the new block and was a pleasant enough room of sufficient size for us not to be crammed together but also not so large that we were going to rattle around like peas in a large pod. In fact ideal sized and I smiled and greeted the other candidates who were already there as I took up my position in the second row as all the front row seats were taken. The room had been laid out with the comfortable but upright chairs which incorporated a table and small desk unit on the side, in two rows of six in a semi circle facing the front so a friendly intimate layout that would no doubt work well for us.

Shortly after I had sat down Belinda came in and peering around looked at the few empty seats still vacant.

I smiled, beckoned and pointed to a seat next to me and she smiled back as she nodded and made her towards where I'd indicated. I took the opportunity to give her a quick look up and down as she did so and noted that her hair which last evening had flowed around her shoulders was today again pulled into a pony tail. No makeup except for a light trace of lipstick but she was dressed in a lightweight cream jumper and smart tight fitting brown jeans. Her feet which were unfettered by hosiery or socks were tucked into some sling back sandals and I enjoyed seeing her bright red toenail varnish. As she sat down there was a slight waft of perfume.

'Good morning again' she said quietly. 'Did you sleep alright?'

'Not bad. Woke a couple of times but soon dropped off again'.

'Lucky you. I went off quickly enough but then I woke around two-ish because I thought there was someone in my room. I was sure I'd heard footsteps but when I put the light on there was nothing. Any rate I got out of bed and although I'd locked the door when I went up I also pushed the bolt across. It took me a while to go off again but I did however then around four o'clock I woke again as I was sure someone had spoken to me. Silly I know but I couldn't help worrying about it and I kind of only dozed from then on until it got light and I got up'.

Now this was interesting as Belinda thought she'd heard something as I had, but before I could engage her in discussion about it the remaining candidates arrived closely followed by Tony and Janet who beamed cheerfully and after waiting for everyone to be seated smiled as they bid us welcome and opened the first session of the four week course.

The morning started with what was effectively a cross between a lecture and a class debate on the subject of the role of senior management. It was cleverly done I thought as it got us into the listening and learning mode but also started to involve us in open discussion. Personally I've never had any real problem with public speaking but obviously some of my fellow attendees were nervous about standing up or indeed sitting and speaking out and they found it a bit of a trying time. However when we broke for coffee at ten thirty everyone had spoken out either through volunteering comments or in response to being asked a direct question by either of our class tutors.

Having the two tutors was also good as it not only kept us on our toes but varied the style of delivery of the lecture. Tony was the more relaxed and peppered his part with a joke or two whereas Janet was more serious and stuck to the primary subject. I don't mean that she was dry or uninteresting. Far from it. It was just different from Tony's method of delivering a lecture. But they were both good and the time went quickly which is always a good sign.

The mid morning coffee break lasted for half an hour and many of the other attendees from other courses being held at the college were milling around getting coffee and biscuits, but as is usually the way at these sorts of things we in our group of twelve kept largely to ourselves as indeed those other people from other courses kept themselves to within their own respective groups. This was how it would be for the duration, as the rapport that we built up was with our own group with whom we were going to be eating, working, arguing, challenging, learning, helping, living and in fact spending virtually all our waking hours with each other. It is a strange hot house sort of atmosphere and sometimes could lead to fearful rows and bust ups between course members and this was something for which the tutors constantly watched out ready to smooth it over or tackle it head on and find a solution if it got nasty.

For the second session we were split up into three groups of four for a project to determine factors affecting motivation of older employees. There had been no pre-selection of who was in which syndicate and Tony had simply waved his arm about to suggest groupings and I was pleased that Belinda was allocated to the same group as me. We and the other two groups were sent off to different and smaller syndicate rooms.

We'd been given an hour to work on the project during which we had to prepare a five minute presentation to give when we were all gathered together again. We worked well as a group and with Peter Chatteris and Raymond King the other two members we listened, suggested, challenged each other's thoughts and suggestions but in a positive and constructive way. Belinda had a quick mind and was clearly going to be an asset to us and although Peter was a bit laid back he did make some good points while Raymond occasionally showed a sudden flash of impatience if his ideas weren't immediately accepted but at least he did accept the collective will of the syndicate. However as it was the first morning we all skated around each other, somewhat willingly conceding points of argument in order to achieve consensus but I was sure that as the weeks progressed things might become quite a bit more difficult.

Peter volunteered to be the spokesman for our little group and give our presentation so we spent the last ten minutes of our allotted time helping him prepare what he was going to say.

We'd just finished when Janet poked her head around the door and asked if we were ready to return to the main lecture room. We were, so we dutifully trooped along the corridor pleased with how our first group syndicate working session had gone.

We were even more pleased a little later as both Tony and Janet were quite fulsome in their praise of what we'd presented. To be fair they also praised the other two syndicate's presentations but I think everyone in the room felt that we'd got the honours for that piece of work.

'Right ho. Then I think you all deserve some lunch so enjoy the culinary delights of the college and please be back here for two o'clock'.

Most of us skipped the bar and went straight into the dining room but I noticed that Raymond when he walked in and sat down had a pint of beer in his hand.

Lunch like breakfast was a buffet and splendid it was too with a choice of three different hot dishes and a huge selection of cold meats, fish, salads and pasta. I helped myself to a small selection of cold meat, with some creamy pasta on the side but I noticed that Belinda just put a mix of salads on her plate.

There was no wine on the table but jugs of water and plenty of brown and white rolls. Finding a table which still had two vacant spaces I nodded to the others there who although from our course were from one of the other syndicates as I sat down. Moments later Belinda asked 'Room for a little one?' and slid into the one remaining space.

The post lunch sessions were divided into two. The one before the mid-afternoon break for tea or coffee wasn't taken by either Tony or Janet but a Professor Jeremy Taylor. He continued with the subject of motivating employees and proved to be an extremely lively and interesting speaker. After the tea break yet another lecturer took her place at the front of the group and Harriet Prime started to discuss the subject of dismissing employees. We had a short syndicate session on this later in the afternoon and again we had to present our findings which both Belinda and I offered to do, so Peter spun a coin and said it was Belinda to do it.

She spoke confidently and presented our syndicate's views clearly and interestingly, but I have to say that I concentrated slightly less on what she was saying and slightly more on studying her body! Her brown jeans fitted closely and demonstrated that she had a neat bum and slim waist and her cream jumper clearly showed the outline of her bra both from the front when she stretched up to point at the easel on which she'd propped the presentation boards she'd produced but also when her back was towards the audience the back strap was also clearly evident.

She finished speaking, was politely and respectfully applauded, questioned by Harriet on a couple of things that she'd said, responded to queries from members of the other two syndicates and finally smiling broadly sat down confident that she'd done a good job. She had and once again we thought that our group had probably produced the best results of the three.

Just before six Harriet finished the session but said she see us again later in the week and she'd just made that point as Tony arrived to take over. After thanking her he enquired generally of all twelve of us whether we'd enjoyed the day, nodded cheerfully when we all unanimously said that we had, grinned as he said 'Well that's a shame and we'll have to see what we can do about it to make the remaining sessions less enjoyable. In fact' he continued 'you might think you've finished for today. Well you'd be wrong! You see here is your assignment for this evening's work which is individual and not syndicate or whole group orientated. You need to work on it alone and then tomorrow morning you will each present your findings, thoughts and proposed action plan to solve the issue raised in the document that I am about to hand out, to the whole group of twelve.

After some discussion of what you say individually we'll put you back in your syndicates to debate the subject and your individual proposals, so we can see how by working together as a small team you might come up with a better solution. Then we'll re-present those syndicate findings to the whole group and re-discuss.

Now that should take the whole of the morning, provided you do your homework properly tonight. Any questions?' and as there were none he started to hand out the assignment brief.

Most like me remained sitting at out little desk units for a while having a quick flick through the four pages we'd been handed then got up and ambled off. I headed for the bar and was soon joined by two or three others and we chatted generally about how we thought the day had gone, what we thought of the lecturers about whom we all agreed they had been excellent, the college and generally started to exchange a little more information about ourselves.

Dinner was served from seven and so a little after six thirty, refusing another beer I went up to my room, showered, changed into some smarter but still casual clothes and was just coming down the stairs into the hall when the gong sounded.

The same two middle aged waitresses who'd served us last night together with two new ones both looking to be in their early twenties that I'd not seen before cheerfully attended to the needs of those dining. By ten past seven the room was full and most places at the various tables were taken. I did a rapid head count and found that there were over eighty people present with only a few empty places. Disappointingly I didn't see Belinda and got on with eating and chatting to my near neighbours whom I'd not met before as they were on a different course and had been here for a week already.

When I had finished as I started to make my way out of the dining room to go to my bedroom to settle down to make a start on studying this project I passed Belinda coming into the room.

'Hi there' I smiled cheerfully. 'The baked halibut which I had is excellent and I can thoroughly recommend it'.

'Thanks' but as she looked a little uneasy I stopped and spoke again.

'Is everything alright?'

'I don't know. I think someone's been into my room as some of my things have been moved around'.

'The maids? You know when they cleaned, tidied and made the beds maybe?'

'No they did that this morning. I'm talking about since lunch. Before the afternoon sessions started I popped up there to freshen up and left a couple of things on the bed and got out this dress to wear this evening which I hung on the side of the wardrobe. But the stuff I left on the bed *and* the dress was on the floor when I went up tonight'.

'Was your window open? It's pretty blustery outside still and perhaps they blew off. After all we're rather high up there on the second floor'.

'No it was shut'.

'Perhaps when you walked out of the room your passing sort of blew them off, or maybe when you shut the door that might have caused a draught. Could that be it?'

'I don't know' then she shrugged gave a rueful smile and said 'You're probably right and as I love fish I'll take your recommendation and have the halibut. Thanks' and with a smile she walked on into the dining room as I made my way upstairs.

There seemed nothing amiss with my room so I settled down in the small armchair, opened the document and started to focus my thoughts and attention to the project we'd been given.

I read it through carefully and discovered that we were to imagine that we'd just arrived as a newly appointed Managing Director of a business known as Troublesome Company Limited. One of the things that was often done on these sorts of courses was to give somewhat odd names to the fictitious companies which we were studying but which clearly depicted what was wrong with them.

So Troublesome was in financial difficulty. Not only was its product range outdated, but its three factories were running well below capacity. A plan had been developed to close one of the factories and re-locate all production into the other two which would be modernised with more up to date machinery. The financial benefits of these changes were detailed in the document. However this plan would result in large scale redundancies of the workforce which the trades union was strongly opposing.

Our task was to firstly define priorities; secondly decide how we were going to persuade the trades union to accept the plan; thirdly produce a new profit and loss schedule showing the benefits of the plan when implemented compared with the existing unsatisfactory P & L, and lastly to decide on a timescale for action.

'Phew' I muttered to myself before adding 'now that's chucking us in at the deep end isn't it?'

The armchair wasn't particularly comfortable but with a bit of wriggling around I soon relaxed as I re-read the document then started to make some notes on immediate thoughts. Time passed and I began developing a plan of action. Moving to the desk unit I started work on the numbers we'd been given and could clearly see the financial benefits for the fictitious company but the task of persuading the trades union was less easy to determine. After all what did they get out of it? Less jobs, fewer people required, reduced overtime earnings and a company less dependent on the goodwill of the union. Eventually though I calculated that if the company shared some of the benefits that it was going to achieve from the changes then they might be able to negotiate union acceptance.

With this thought now burning in my mind I developed a proposition to raise the wage rate for those employees that would be retained; planned a phased programme of redundancies and structured an enhanced package of financial benefits for those that would leave. All in all it seemed to me that in this theoretical world it would work fine. Tomorrow I'd discover whether what I'd planned would be considered sensible and a way forward or whether I'd be laughed out of court.

I was about to finish by establishing my priorities for action and create a timescale for making it all happen both of which were required by the brief when I got the distinct feeling that someone was looking over my shoulder as I was sure I could feel breathing on my neck.

Swinging round there was no-one there of course but I again thought I heard footsteps moving across the floor. I stood up and walked over to the door which I noticed was slightly ajar although I knew I'd shut it firmly when I came up. Closing it for some reason I gave a shiver as suddenly the room felt cold but mentally deciding that it was because the door had somehow opened and let in cold air from the corridor I went to a drawer and extracted a lightweight sweater which I pulled on. Returning to the desk I finished off my work for the evening although I have to admit that once or twice I couldn't stop myself glancing over my shoulder but on each occasion nothing was there.

A final check through what I'd prepared and I thought

that would do for the evening's work and glancing at my watch I saw that it was approaching ten o'clock.

Putting my papers and work away in the folder I left the room being sure to properly shut and lock the door and made my way downstairs to the tv lounge where I dropped into an armchair, which incidentally was large and much more comfortable than the smaller one in the my room, and in company with a number of others in the room watched the ten o'clock news.

When that finished I strongly felt that the bar was calling to me so I was soon getting happily acquainted with a delightful pint of bitter. A little later I was about to order another when Belinda came in, smiled at me and opening her handbag extracted her purse and asked what I wanted to drink? Refusing her offer I bought her a whisky and ginger ale and another pint for myself.

'How are you getting on with Troublesome then?' I enquired.

'I'd fire the whole lot and move lock stock and barrel to China to have their products made' she chuckled in reply.

'Hey I don't think that's the answer they want?'

'No I know, but it might be fun to suggest it and see what the tutors say and do as a result' she laughed. 'How did you get on with it?'

So I told her what I'd worked out and where I'd got to with my solutions and we chatted for a while until she said that she'd started to work in her room but felt uncomfortable and so had come down to one of the syndicate rooms in the new block and carried on with her project in there.

'I think this old house is a really spooky place' she

announced 'and I really don't like being up there on the second floor. Do you know I think it's only you and me up there? Everyone else is on the first floor or in the other newer building. I feel as though I'm being watched up there all the time and I'm still not happy about the way my things had moved earlier today and tonight when I went up after supper I'm sure I locked my door when I went down but it was unlocked and open. Do you think there are ghosts up there?'

In an attempt to reassure her I snorted that of course there weren't but even as I said it I wasn't wholly certain that I was right and later when I said that I was going up she quickly finished her drink and asked me to walk her to her room.

From her expression it was clear that it wasn't an invitation to go and sleep with her and it seemed a genuine request just to accompany her to her door. I duly complied, wished her goodnight, watched as she went into her room, waited until I heard the key turn in the lock, called out 'Goodnight, sleep well' and wandered down the corridor to my own room.

She was right it was a dreary spooky old place up here but I was soon in my own room, locked the door, undressed and in bed where I tossed and turned for ages as I thought about the feelings I had earlier that someone was looking over my shoulder and just as I was almost asleep once again, I definitely heard footsteps going across the room. Quickly switching on the light I saw nothing but the sound of walking ceased immediately but shortly after I'd switched the light off again and snuggled down I was sure I heard them again.

'Piss off and let me get to sleep' I snapped and I didn't

hear another sound until sometime later when I was fast asleep a loud banging on my door woke me with a real start.

'Greg please open up and let me in' called a voice which I recognised as Belinda.

'Alright hang on' I replied as I scrambled out of bed and finding my boxers which I'd hung over the back of the chair when I undressed I quickly tugged them on, unlocked and opened the door to Belinda who was wearing pale pink silky pyjamas, bare foot and clearly very distressed by something.

'Oh thank God. Can I come in?' and without waiting for an answer she pushed her way inside and plonked down on my bed.

'Hey whatever's the matter?'

'There's someone or something in my room. I know there is. I hear voices, sounds of footsteps and breathing. I am so frightened I just had to get out but I couldn't face going downstairs like this. Can I stay here for a bit? Please?'

'Sure' I muttered as I rubbed my face to wake myself up. 'Look would you like a coffee or a cup of tea perhaps?'

'A bloody great whisky might do me better' she replied weakly 'but yes tea would be great. Thank you'.

I took my bath robe off the hook behind the door and wrapped it around me then I collected the kettle and the one tea cup provided in the room, went into the bathroom where I filled the kettle and rinsed the cup then returned to the bedroom where Belinda was still sitting exactly where she'd been before I left, unmoving and staring straight ahead. I knelt down beside the desk unit, plugged in the kettle and then turned back to her.

'I don't think I can stay up here anymore' she sniffed as a tear ran down her cheek.

'Well you don't have to go right away, have your tea first' I responded a little puzzled by exactly what she meant.

'No I don't mean that. I mean I can't go on using my room. I think it's haunted. Have you read the booklet about this place? It says that there are ghosts'.

'It says there have been some reports of ghosts' I corrected 'and yes I have. Interestingly I have also heard or felt something strange in here'.

'You have?' she exclaimed eyes wide. 'What here in your room?'

'Uh huh I thought while I was working on my project that someone was looking over my shoulder. I feel that I've also heard or imagined footsteps in here and like you also the sound of breathing'.

'Oh my God' she muttered looking anxiously around the room. 'What in here?'

'Yes'.

At that point the kettle reached boiling point so I made her a cup of tea in the only tea cup provided and made myself a coffee in the water glass.

'Cheers' I grinned.

'God I'm not usually a wimp or pathetic like this but to be honest Greg I am really frightened. You remember that I said my things had been moved about. Well I'm sure they had again this evening. What the hell am I going to do?'

'First thing in the morning go and see someone.

Maybe Janet could help get you relocated into another room on a different floor or into the new block?'

'Yes' she nodded 'that's a good idea but what about the rest of tonight?'

'Well why don't you take my bed and I'll sleep in the armchair?'

'Would you really let me do that? You don't mind?'

Actually I minded a great deal as I'm a chap who needs a good eight hours sleep a night and I doubted if I'd get much sleep in that chair and would at best doze off and on but I'd made the offer and that was that.

'No not at all. I'll be fine in the chair'.

'Do you think this is why there aren't many people up here on this second floor? Because it's haunted I mean? Just you and me' she asked in a quiet voice.

'No idea but maybe. Right now finish your tea and then let's try out our communal sleeping arrangements' I grinned much more cheerfully than I felt.

'You are sure?' she asked in a small voice.

'Yes go on hop in. Hey you don't snore do you' I laughed as she stood up, put the now empty tea cup down on the little bedside unit, lifted the duvet and swung her legs underneath and then pulling it up to her chin snuggled down before turning her head to look across at me.

'No of course I don't snore!' she snapped quietly but with a little smile.

'How do you know or has your boyfriend told you that you don't?' I chuckled.

'I don't have a boyfriend, well not at the moment but I just know that I don't'.

'How?' I queried as I took off my bathrobe and pulled

on a pair of trousers, a tee shirt, a pair of socks and a sweater.

'Because'.

'Because isn't a proper answer' I mocked.

''Well it's my answer and the only one you're getting' and she watched as I pulled the desk chair out to be in front of the armchair so I could rest my feet on it. Then I took the spare blanket out of the wardrobe and wrapped it around myself as I wriggled down into the armchair finally spreading my bathrobe on top of me.

'Right can you turn the bedside light out?' I said quietly. 'Good night'.

'Good night and thank you again'.

'You're welcome' and as the light went out I sat in the armchair staring into the darkness reflecting on several things. Firstly the odd noises and feeling that we'd both experienced and I have to say that if the place was haunted and Belinda moved away from this floor that I really didn't fancy being up here all by myself. Secondly I was also conscious that when I'd taken off my bathrobe to pull on some clothes she had looked quite intently at my almost naked body and lastly she herself had looked really cute and fetching in her silky pyjamas.

'It was my fiancé' her soft voice came out of the darkness.

'What was your fiancé?'

'Who told me' she sniggered.

'Told you what?'

'That I don't snore'.

'I didn't know you were engaged?'

'I'm not any more. We broke it off last year'.

'Sorry to hear that'.

'Umm so was I at the time but these things happen. Good night'.

As I sat there trying to find the least uncomfortable position I couldn't help but listen for any ghostly noises but all seemed quiet and soon the only sound that I heard was Belinda's quiet breathing.

I did drop off and dozed but I woke several times feeling stiff and aching . However she was calm and quiet in my bed and as dawn eventually crept across the sky the room gradually lighted so I could watch her face relaxed and still as she slept and I decided that she really was rather pretty.

At seven I clambered out of the chair and went into the bathroom where I refilled the little kettle and soon had it boiling away so using the last teabag and sachet of powdered milk provided I made her another cup of tea which I put on the bedside table as I looked down at her still fast asleep. The duvet had moved down and her chest was exposed and I could clearly see the outline of a nipple through the material of her pyjama jacket. Nice I thought and resisting the temptation to stroke or touch it I gently shook her shoulder.

'Hello. Your early morning tea madam' I grinned as she opened her eyes which momentarily widened in sudden alarm but that expression was replaced almost immediately by a look of understanding as she obviously remembered where she was and why.

'Oh hello. Thank you. That's really kind. Did you manage to get any sleep?' she asked as she sat up pulling the duvet to her chin.

'Yes no problem at all. Slept like the proverbial log thanks. Now I'm going to go and have a swim to freshen me up before I get shaved and dressed. Fancy an early morning dip?'

'Yes why not? Sounds like a great idea. Let me finish this' she added waving the cup then I'll get my swimming things from my room. Oh look, would you come to my room with me while I do that?'

'An invite to a pretty lady's bedroom? Now that is an offer I couldn't possibly refuse' I joked.

She smiled and took another sip of tea. 'Were there any, you know, any other noises or anything after I went to sleep?' she asked slightly nervously.

'No only the sound of your snoring' I smiled.

'Liar! Hey I don't do I?'

'Oh an absolutely deafening row which kept me awake for ages'.

'That is so not true. You just said you slept like a log'.

We smiled at each other as she swung her legs out of my bed and stood up. 'Will you come with me to my room please?'

'I told you it was an offer I couldn't refuse. Yes of course' and unlocking my door I held it aside for her and she walked out into the corridor as I followed enjoying the view of her bum as it moved inside the pyjama trousers, I wished that we were going to her room for a bout of sex as she was very attractive and I have to say that I was getting to quite fancy her. Oh well I thought there's still the best part of four weeks here yet so you never know your luck. She stopped outside her door and gingerly pushed it open.

'Here let me check it for you' I said as I moved in front, walked inside and peered around. 'Nothing here that shouldn't be as far as I can see' I called back to her so she followed me into her room which was identical to mine. Same size, same furniture, same bed, same everything, except that scattered about were lots of feminine things. Makeup, handbag, a tee shirt draped over the armchair with a pale blue bra on top of it while on the floor in the corner a pair of lacy matching panties which she'd obviously discarded when she undressed last night.

'I just need to use the bathroom' she said as she went inside that little room and shut the door. I sat down on her desk chair and seeing her folder on the desk couldn't help myself from lifting the cover and peeking inside but all I saw were lots of scribbled notes. I turned a page and there was a heading KEY POINTS with many different headings but at that point I heard the chain next door flush, so shutting the folder I swung round so I was looking into the room as she re-emerged brushing her hair and winding it into a pony tail.

'My swim stuff is in here' she said as she opened a drawer in the chest of drawers and moments later she was holding what looked like the two parts of a bikini making me glad that I'd invited her to join me for the swim. 'Do you think they've got towels in the pool area or shall I take mine from here?'

'No they've got some there. I saw a notice about it when I was having a look around on Sunday after I arrived. Right got everything then?'

Going back into the bathroom she soon returned with the bathrobe wrapped around her, a small towel over her arm and wearing her open toed sandals that she'd worn yesterday.

'Yep got everything' she agreed.

We went back to my room where I collected my own swimming trunks. 'You've put your costume on have you?' I asked. She nodded. 'Ok do you want to wait in the corridor while I do the same?'

'Erm will you leave your door open a bit so ……..'

'So you can peep in and get a cheap thrill from watching me stripping off?' I chuckled.

'No so I can call for help if I get frightened'.

'Sure' and so I did as requested. The door was open but she stood a little to the side of it and a few moments later I walked out also in bathrobe, trunks beneath and some flip flops on my feet.

Arriving at the pool area we separated into the respective ladies and gents changing rooms and met up again on the poolside. Again her glance flicked up and down my body as it had last night but my own look at her was more languid as she looked simply stunning.

The bikini was multicoloured and quite small. The bra part left quite a lot of breast tissue exposed and the matching pants were not only high legged but rather skimpy at the front although when she turned to walk to the end of the pool her bottom looked delightful as it was well covered, not split by just a thin thong and the varied colours and pattern contrasted well with her skin.

'Race you to the end' she smiled as she stood looking at the water and staring down the pool. 'Ready, steady, go' and we both dived in and swam to the far end which we reached almost simultaneously. 'Four length race?' she announced.

'Ok. Start us off'.

So she did. Now I am a good swimmer but so was she and although I beat her it wasn't by much and I had to work hard to do that. Puffing and laughing we stood in the shallow end holding onto the rail.

'Right now I'm going to do some lengths but in a bit more of a leisurely pace' I stated then pushed off and swam up and down at a reasonable but non racing speed. I swam for about ten minutes and when I finished I hauled myself out of the water and saw that she was sitting on one of the benches that were located against the wall along the side of the pool and I have to say that she looked quite stunning in her wet bikini and with her dark hair still dripping wet.

'You're a really good swimmer Greg aren't you?'

'Not bad' I admitted. 'Right are we off back upstairs now?'

'Yes' and her face which had looked quite relaxed suddenly appeared tense.

'Look. Let's meet outside the changing area and then if it'll put your mind at rest when we get upstairs you can come and wait in my room while I have a quick shower and shave and then I'll come and join you in your room while you do whatever you have to do to appear dressed and beautiful to face the day' I smiled.

'Thank you' and her gratitude was obvious.

A little while later both now dressed we made our way to the dining room and had breakfast then as soon as we finished eating and checking her watch while once again looking tense Belinda spoke.

'I'm going to try and find Janet. Would you come with me to sort of back me up as it were?'

'Sure' and we left the room together and headed to our main lecture room where fortunately she'd just arrived.

'Hi there' she smiled cheerily. 'How do you get on with last night's project? Any problems?'

'Not with the project but yes I've got a problem, and a big one at that?' said Belinda with a serious expression on her face. 'Look Janet I know this is going to sound stupid but I want to change to a different room as I think that mine is' she paused and looked slightly sheepish 'umm, well I think it's haunted'.

Janet looked at her and then at me. 'Which room are you in?'

'Two oh six'.

'Second floor?'

'Yes'.

'They shouldn't be using the second floor for bedrooms. We've had problems up there before'.

'You have?'

'Yes sounds, footsteps, various things have been reported. Even some of the chambermaids won't go up there to service and clean those rooms. The college is not supposed to put people on that floor now. They must have either made a mistake or be full up everywhere else'.

'I think they're full elsewhere as when I checked in they said they were full and allocated me a room up there too' I added trying to assist.

'You are on the second floor as well?'

I nodded.

'Do you want to move?'

'Well I'm sure I've heard things as well, so if there was a vacant room somewhere else then yes I think that I might prefer to move'.

'Right come on' and Janet immediately marched Belinda and me straight off to the college office which was at the back of the building on the ground floor. Demanding to know why we had been allocated rooms on the second floor she told the administrator that we were to move and for her to find us rooms either on the first floor or in the new building.

'No rooms at all vacant in the new building and we're short of eight rooms here on the first floor as they're being re-decorated' responded the somewhat sulky woman who'd been the one that checked me in on Sunday.

'No vacant rooms at all then?' enquired Janet somewhat testily.

'No'.

'Well you'll have to find some. You know you're not supposed to put course attendees up there on the second floor'.

'Can't help it there's nowhere else for them to go'.

'What about the guest lecturer's rooms?'

'They're for visiting lecturers who need to stay the night. I can't allocate them'.

'How many of them are there?'

'Six'.

'And how many are presently occupied?'

'One'.

'Well there you are then you've got five empty rooms. Kindly allocate two of those to these two people'.

If looks could have killed then Janet would have dropped dead on the floor there and then from the venomous glare the administrator gave to our potential saviour.

'They might be empty now but we've got three lecturers coming this afternoon and they'll be required for them'.

'Still leaves two'.

'No it doesn't as the College Principle's son is coming tomorrow to stay for a few days when he's back from the army' she snapped with a triumphant look on her face.

'Look stop prevaricating will you. I've got lectures to take in a few minutes and I want to get this sorted out before I leave to do that. To my mind it's simple. You have stupidly taken eight rooms out of use to decorate. How many are being worked on at the same time? One or two I imagine so you could have left the others in use but you didn't. However you have got one empty room so I insist that at least one of these two candidates has that and I think you should bring back into usage some of the rooms that are scheduled for decoration and then my other candidate can be moved'. The two women stared at each other for a moment so Janet added 'Or I'll ring the college principle right now and tell him how incompetent and unhelpful you are. Hand me that phone please' and still seeing a stubborn look on the face of the recipient of her demands she repeated 'Either make the arrangements on that computer or give me the phone *now*'.

'Alright no need to take that attitude' muttered the hapless seated woman sulkily as she started to tap at the computer keyboard. 'I'll see what I can do about the rooms being decorated but in the meantime I'll allocate the vacant room to one of these two. So who is going to have it then?'

'You take it' I said to Belinda 'and if another room becomes vacant I'll move then'.

'Are you sure?' she enquired but nevertheless looked very grateful.

'Yes of course'.

'Thanks' then turning to Janet and the administrator she added 'I'll move my things in the lunch hour'.

We all stood and watched as the administrator grunted and tapped the keyboard then in a couple of minutes she looked at Belinda and said 'Right you are now in room one forty six which is a nice room in the south wing' she sniffed 'double in fact. We've only got two double rooms and that's one of them. Key will be in the door but bring the key from your present second floor room back here when you've changed over. Anything else?' and she looked up at Janet.

'No you've been most helpful. Thank you' and turning on her heel she spoke addressing both Belinda and me. 'Ok I must dash now but do let me know as soon as Sheila' and she looked at the administrator whose name I now knew as unusually she wasn't wearing a name badge 'organises a different room for you. Any other problems just let me know and I hope you are comfortable in your new rooms' and with that she did literally dash off while Belinda and I walked more sedately back into the hallway.

'I need to get my stuff for this morning's sessions' I muttered.

'So do I so can we go together?'

'Of course' and the two of us climbed both staircases to the second floor went into our rooms, collected our papers and documents and felt relieved when we walked back down into the lecture room where all the other ten course members were already seated and Tony was obviously waiting for us to join them as looking at his watch he greeted us and bid us welcome.

CHAPTER 3

The morning's work went well and at lunch time I stood guard for Belinda as she moved her things from the second floor down to her new room on the first floor and as the old bat who'd grudgingly re-allocated her to here had said it was a lovely room. Bright, cheerful with a nice view over the college lawns and being a double room it was so much larger than the rather pokey little singles that we'd been in before. However as I looked around it dawned on me then that I would now be the only one up on the second floor and that was a prospect that didn't at all fill me with delight.

We had two syndicate projects in the afternoon and then a general class discussion on what we'd learnt from them, after which we were handed our evening study assignment.

This stated that we were to imagine we'd just been joined a new company as a senior human resources manager but the company had some people problems as it had recently taken over a competitor and was now in the process of integrating two completely different management styles. One was autocratic - tell the employees what was required and then drive hard to force them to do it. The other was democratic - lots of mutual problem solving, team working and helping each other achieve results.

Our task was to decide how to integrate the two styles, define what training needs would be required and also in selecting a deputy to ourself, whether we would chose someone from the autocratic or the democratic company, and why we made the choice that we did?

It sounded an interesting task and after stopping for a quick half of bitter in the bar I went up to my room. I have to say that my cheerful feelings disappeared as I went up the second flight of curving stairs and along the gloomy corridor but when I got to my room for a moment then the doom and gloom from outside disappeared as the room seemed calm, quiet and reasonably well lit unlike the corridor outside.

I showered and changed then left my papers on the desk unit and decided to go downstairs for a walk through the grounds, have another beer, eat dinner and then I would work on the assignment later.

The bar was quite a jolly place and we all chatted about the task that we'd been given and started to exchange ideas and thoughts. Some were quite open and forthcoming while others were more reticent and surprisingly reluctant to discuss and share their views.

The dinner gong sounded and I looked around and saw Belinda walking into the dining room so I swerved over towards her and we sat together. When our choice of meal had been served and we'd started to eat I asked 'Settled into your new room ok?'

'You changed rooms?' queried Jason another member of our course who was sitting opposite her.

'Yes I wasn't too happy with the one that they'd given me so they've kindly relocated me'.

'You're in this old house aren't you?'

'Uh huh'.

'Glad I'm in the new block. It's great there with every mod con but I believe things are a bit more spartan here. Hey' he said leaning forward and blatantly staring down Belinda's obvious and not uninteresting cleavage 'if you want to change rooms again and would like to share my lonely little bed where we could run through each other's projects and ideas as well as finding other interesting things to do with each other I'd be more than happy to oblige'.

I was about to intervene to help her from this guy but she glanced at me giving the slightest shake of her head, then looked quickly around the room and smiling at him reached out and took his hand.

'Jason I'm not sure how many men there are here on courses at this college, possibly fifty maybe even more but I'd just like you to know that *if* I wanted a man to share my bed tonight which I certainly *don't*, then you'd be right at the end of the line with all those other men *well* in front of you. So put your dirty little insinuations and thoughts back into that cesspit that you call a mind and forget it' and smiling sweetly she patted his hand a couple of times before adding 'I do hope that's quite clear' then she picked up her knife and fork and started to eat again.

'No need to take that attitude' he muttered 'just having a bit of fun'.

'You might call it fun but I think I'd call it rather pathetic' she snapped then giving me a wink she turned to the person on her other side and started to talk about tonight's project.

After we'd eaten we decamped to the coffee room and Belinda, Peter Chatteris, Raymond King and I got ourselves into a little group huddle where we talked about the course so far, and a little about tonight's project. Peter who was often quite open in discussions had some interesting thoughts which I tucked away in the back of my mind but after about half an hour or so we all mutually decided to break up and go our separate ways to work on our own as instructed, but we agreed to meet up again at ten o'clock as we thought that we'd have had enough of solus working by then and would welcome a beer or two and some relaxed company.

I went upstairs and got my files and the project paper and went back downstairs again where I found a small syndicate room called Maple that was empty and I settled down in there at the table and became engrossed in the work on which I made quick and I thought good progress. I suppose it was after about an hour that I looked up as the door had opened and closed again but no-one had come in and there was no-one in the room except me.

'Oh for God's sake' I chided myself 'stop imagining things will you' and I settled down to work again but even as I did so I glanced around every now and then as I could feel a presence in the room, or at least I thought that I did but nothing else transpired and when I'd finished all that I wanted to do tonight and seeing from the clock on the mantelpiece that it was ten past ten, I closed my folder, gathered up my papers, files and notes and walked back to the bar.

It was quite busy and conversation flowed brightly and cheerfully. Harry the bar man was efficient, quick at serving and produced a pint of bitter for me in no time, after I'd ordered.

'Pay now or want a tab opened?' he asked.

'Open me a tab please as I'll probably have another'.

'Here Greg if you're ordering then mine's a pint as well' laughed Raymond as he came to the bar and put an arm around my shoulders. A couple of others from our course who'd just arrived added their requirements to the order and it was just as I was signing for the three additional drinks that Belinda walked in and up to the bar.

'Good evening Miss and what's it to be?' queried Harry.

'A gin and tonic please'.

'Can I get that for you?'

'No thanks' she smiled at me in response to my enquiry 'but you can join me if you like as I've got a query on our evening homework' and so we took ourselves off to a quiet corner and chatted about the project. After a while and having discussed and I think helped her with her query I got myself another beer but she refused a second g & t.

We talked about our respective employers, our jobs, our taste in music and just generally enjoyed each other's company until around eleven thirty we agreed it was time to go to bed and so we walked into the hallway and up the first flight of stairs then said goodnight as I continued on up the second flight.

'Thanks for a nice evening Greg' she called up to me.

'Pleasure. I enjoyed it too'.

'Hope you sleep ok up there'.

'So do I' and the fervency of my reply was deeply meant.

However after I got into bed and had laid for a few minutes thinking about Belinda and what a trim body she had including that cleavage apart from some sounds of whispering which I put down to the wind outside nothing disturbed me and I dropped off to sleep.

Exactly what time it was I don't know when I was jerked awake by the sound of screaming. It was very loud, continuous and the screams were interspersed with the words "Fire, fire".

I shot out of bed as not only could I distinctly smell smoke but there were loud crackling sounds of the type that a fire makes when wood is burning. Quickly I switched on the light and rushed outside into the corridor where the sound immediately ceased and the smell of smoke was gone. There was nothing. The corridor was empty, quiet and gloomy. Tentatively I peered back into my room but there was nothing there now either. I put my head inside the room and all was quiet.

'God what a dream' I said to myself as I went back inside, locked the door and got back into bed but no sooner had I settled down than I smelt smoke again. This was very worrying but as I again switched on the bedside light there was no smoke to be seen, the smoke detector blinking its little red light to show that it was working correctly hadn't gone off and this time there was no crackling sound or screaming.

I lay for a moment or two wondering what to do. If there was a fire somewhere in the building I could be trapped up here on the second floor. But if I sounded the fire alarm and there was nothing then everyone was going to be pretty pissed off with me for disturbing them in the middle of the night for no reason.

Once again I went out into the corridor and prowled about. I opened several doors to other rooms which of course I knew were unoccupied but there was nothing. They were empty, furnished like my own room but devoid of any people in there. When I got to the room that Belinda had used I went inside and peered around then sat on her bed for a few minutes as she'd said that she'd heard things but there was nothing this evening. Maybe whatever it was had moved out of her room as she was no longer there and moved into my room.

I continued to stalk along the corridor and went right to the end, checking every room but there was nothing untoward and no sound or sight of any semblance of fire. No smoke, no crackling, no screaming. On the way back to my own room I again looked into each empty room then returned to mine, shut and locked the door before getting back into bed.

I lay very tensely waiting for something to happen but nothing did. All remained quiet, still and peaceful so I decided that I'd stop imagining things and go to sleep and I was almost asleep when I heard a woman giggling. For a moment I thought that it might be Belinda playing a trick on me, so I called out 'Hey Belinda is that you?' but she didn't reply and the giggling continued.

Somehow giggling wasn't as threatening as footsteps and definitely not as worrying as screams or shouts of "Fire". I then wondered if maybe there was a woman giggling in a another room and that somehow the sound was being transmitted to my room, through a water pipe or along an electricity duct perhaps?

But it still continued and I worked out that there was more than one person giggling. Sometimes it seemed that there were two gigglers and then I thought that maybe there were three. That was when the voices started and I distinctly heard a woman's voice say "Ooh sir that is so naughty of you" followed by the same voice I think, but it could have been another, saying "Go on then sir have your way with me, I won't stop you".

What and who was speaking?

Getting out of bed again I prowled around my room listening carefully more intrigued than frightened but although I could vaguely hear whispers the words were too indistinct to determine what was being said. However when I got back into bed then the sound of the voices seemed louder and I could pick out words and phrases again as well as more giggles.

"Aah that's wonderfully wicked"; "If you really want to"; I've never done that sir"; "Ooh that is so lovely".

There were more words and phrases and then a man's voice saying "Come here wench" followed by more female giggling, but after that I could only get part words and eventually I grew tired of listening especially as slowly but continuously the voices faded away until I could hear them no more.

Thanking my lucky stars that I might be left in peace I snuggled down in bed but determined that I was somehow or other going to insist on a change of room tomorrow and be re-located onto the first floor or into the new block.

Once again I was almost asleep when the screams started again louder than ever. "Fire fire. Heavens above the house is afire" and the room was reeking of smoke and the crackling sounds were all around.

This time I didn't wait and was out of bed in one bound and ran along the corridor, down the stairs checking as I went that there was no sign of actual smoke, no wisps seeping anywhere and no sounds of burning or crackling.

On the main landing at the top of the first flight up from the huge hallway a long way below there were three corridors leading off with arrows showing room numbers pointing to specific corridors. For a moment I couldn't remember the number I wanted, then it came to me so ignoring 100 - 116 and 117 -132, I ran down the third corridor marked 133 – 150 and stopped outside 146.

I knocked and then knocked again more loudly and soon I heard sounds of movement from inside.

'Who is it?' came her voice.

'Belinda it's me Greg. Please can I come in for a minute'.

'Greg?'

'Yes open up. Please'.

I heard the lock turn and then the door opened and she stood there in a knee length red trimmed with white nightdress, her hair tousled, and on her face which was shiny with no makeup there was a puzzled expression.

'I ......'

'Come in' and she stood aside. 'Is it noises up there in your room?'

'Yes. There's been screaming .....'

'Screaming?' she enquired with a worried look on her face.

'Yes really loud and dreadful screaming and shouts of fire and I could hear women giggling and whispering and talking and a man's voice. I can't stay up there tonight. Can I borrow a chair in here?'

'Oh course' then she looked at me. Go into the bathroom I want to change'.

'Eh?'

'Just do it if you want to stay here tonight!'

So I did as she asked and a few minutes later she opened the bathroom door and said 'It's ok you can come back out now' and as I did I saw that she'd changed into pyjamas.

'Right now look as well as this proper bed there's a put-you-up bed in the corner. You can sleep on that if you like'.

Looking at where she was pointing I saw that there was a folded up temporary bed the sort many people have tucked away in their homes for an unexpected overnight guest, which I guess is what I was for Belinda tonight.

'Great' I exclaimed as I wheeled it away from the wall and folded it down into place creating a low narrow little bed complete with a thin mattress.

'Now you'd better put something over you if that's all you've got here' she chucked and it was at that moment that I realised that I was just in my boxers.

'Oh God sorry I just ran. I was so keen to get out I didn't stop to think about dressing'.

'No matter. I quite like having an almost naked man banging on my door in the middle of the night as long as it isn't that creep Lucas' she laughed and as she did so her eyes ran down, lingered on my crotch area then traversed back up my body. 'Look I'm quite warm enough with the duvet and there are a couple of blankets in the wardrobe. You can also have my bathrobe to wrap round you. I think with that lot you should be alright don't you?'

'Yes thanks' and shortly I was wearing her robe and tucking the blankets around me as I wriggled about trying to get cosy on the somewhat lumpy and distinctly uncomfortable little bed. However after we'd said good night and she'd turned out the light I lay for a while enjoying the smell of the perfume which emanated from her bathrobe as I guessed that the last time this had been worn it would probably have been wrapped around her naked body and with that happy and somewhat erotic thought I fell asleep not waking until she shook my shoulder several hours later asking 'Are you swimming this morning?'

'Yes' but then I realised I was on the first floor and all I had on were my pants. 'Can I borrow your robe to go to my room and get changed and then I'll return here, give you back your robe and we can go together to the pool.

So that's what we did and to my relief all was calm and quiet in my room.

After breakfast I went to find Sheila the administrator who grudgingly admitted that there was now a vacant room on the first floor as one of those being decorated was finished and thus serviceable again so clutching the key to my new room number 108, I went to the lecture room and settled down to the morning's work or projects, lectures and syndicate working.

At lunchtime Belinda accompanied me to my room and we quickly cleared my stuff into a suitcase and a carrier bag and then we went to my newly allocated room. As we dumped the stuff on the bed, she said 'I even felt nervous for the few minutes that we were in that creepy room of yours' and I admitted that I had too and that furthermore I was extremely glad to be out of there for the rest of the time that I was due to spend at Windsor Management College.

***

So the course continued. I slept well in my new room.

There were no extraneous noises. I had undisturbed night's sleep.

Our syndicate team were consistently best in the marks and positions awarded by the tutors and at the end of the first week a little before six o'clock on the Saturday evening we were all assembled in the class lecture room as Tony and Janet smiled at us from the front.

'Right' said Tony 'you've survived the first week and I have to tell you that I think you've all done very well individually and in your syndicate teams. Now you may remember when you arrived that we promised you all that at the end of each week the winning syndicate would be given the enormous prize of a bottle of champers and so it gives us great pleasure to award that to syndicate one. So will Belinda, Peter, Raymond and Greg come out to accept their winning bottle and have their photograph taken?'

There was some cheerful ribbing from the other eight course members of the other two syndicates but also some genuine applause and both Janet and Tony were sincere in their words of congratulation.

'However we must warn you that next week the work gets tougher and you will have some longer projects one of which will run over two days however before that we have some good news for you all don't we Janet?'

'Indeed we do. Firstly there is no project work for you tonight'. She paused as there were cries of "Great" or "Hooray" then continued 'and the second piece of good news is that tomorrow is Sunday and there is no college work for you then either until we all re-convene again at five o'clock in the afternoon when we'll discuss next week's work and hand you out your evening homework for that night which will be a self study project.

Now I know that it may be hard for you to imagine but from this moment on' and theatrically looking at her watch then grinning she added 'you are welcome to do whatever you wish this evening and all day tomorrow until five. You are free to relax and enjoy all the many varied and excellent the facilities of the college, but at five o'clock tomorrow we will reconvene in here and the work for next week will re-start.

So thanks everyone for all your hard work during this first week. I believe you've worked well individually, in your syndicate teams and as a whole class'.

Tony then took up his position in the centre of the room and closed the session with a few words. 'Good show and well done everyone. Enjoy your night and day off and return here to this room tomorrow refreshed, relaxed and ready for another week's learning. Oh and by the way we're going to mix you up so that you'll all be in different syndicates next week' and with a grin he indicated that the day's sessions were over.

We all filed out of the lecture room and most of us headed for the bar where we were soon happily ensconced with drinks in our hands gleefully reflecting on the joy of a free evening and a free day tomorrow.

Belinda was to one side of the room chatting to Raymond and a couple of women from another course. After a few minutes I made my way across to her and I noted again what a lovely smile she had as she greeted me. Waiting until there was a gap in the conversation I leaned forward and said quietly 'As we've a free evening do you fancy escaping from Colditz for tonight and sneaking off somewhere to find a restaurant as a change from eating here?'

'What a lovely idea. Give me half an hour to have a bath and change and I'll meet you by the reception desk at' she paused to glance at her watch 'seven? Will that be ok?'

'That'll be fine' and with a real feeling of delight I watched as she excused herself from the others and walked out of the bar her tight jeans accentuating her neat bum lines.

Knowing that I was going to be driving I sipped my pint slowly while joining in the conversation around me but with about twenty minutes to go before I was due to meet Belinda I also excused myself, went to the dining room register and signed myself and her out from eating tonight, and ran up the stairs to my first floor room to have a quick shower and change including dabbing some aftershave on my cheeks, wrists and a squirt down my open necked shirt onto my chest.

I was waiting downstairs in the hallway when she came down and as she reached the bottom she smiled, did a twirl and asked 'Am I ok like this?'

'Very ok' I grinned quickly looking her up and down and enjoying the way that her loose skirt which came to just above her knees had swirled out as she spun round exposing about another six inches or perhaps a little more of her legs. 'Come on' and leading the way I set off across the car park to where I'd parked six days ago.

Good grief is that all it was? It seemed that I'd been at the college forever! As we reached the car having blipped to unlock it I did the gentlemanly bit and held open the passenger door for her to get in and then quickly walked round to my side and soon had started the vehicle and was driving slowly out of the car park.

'Do you know this area at all?'

'No I haven't a clue. I used my sat-nav to find the place but I've never been to Norfolk before. It seemed to be a hell of a long way from Bristol though' she replied just as we arrived at the end of the drive which led onto a country lane.

Reaching into my pocket I extracted a pound coin and handed it to her. 'Heads we go left, tails we go right so spin the coin and determine where our route will lead us'.

She spun the coin but dropped it and even though I switched on the inside light she spent a couple of minutes scrabbling around in the car interior until she eventually found it.

'Which way is it to be then?' I asked.

'It's tails, so I guess that means we go to the right'.

We did and set off enjoying the freedom of being out of the college. We both remarked that we felt as though we were either playing truant or had escaped from a prison and it was a nice feeling. We'd been driving for about fifteen minutes when we came to a small village straggling along the main road and as we passed through at the far end was a pub that looked immediately welcoming. It had notices outside indicating that it served food and looking at Belinda I checked whether she was happy for us to try there for a meal. She was and so soon we were walking into the bar where the landlady to our delight confirmed that they still had some tables free.

The whole place looked so welcoming and inviting with traditional real oak beams, winking horse brasses, a lovely fire burning in the huge fireplace and a real cheerful feeling of warmth and happiness and we immediately felt that we'd made a good choice for the evening. I ordered a glass of white wine for her while I chose one of the non alcoholic lagers that they had behind the bar.

We took our drinks and sat by the fire but after a few minutes both decided that we were far too hot there and so we moved to a different part of the bar where we studied the menu and decided what to order.

I caught the eye of the waitress, a chubby girl with a name badge of Kerrie and we ordered. Belinda chose house pate followed by grilled plaice while I plumped for crayfish tails and avocado in a mild curry mayonnaise to kick off and then a steak with salad as my main course.

The evening was a great success. We both relaxed in each other's company spoke about our early lives, upbringing, schooling and careers to date.

We also talked hesitantly at first and then with more confidence about the strange happenings at the college on the second floor. We compared notes as to exactly what we'd each heard and speculated as to what could be the cause. Neither of us was really prepared to admit to believing in ghosts and yet after some considerable debate on the matter we came to the conclusion that there was probably no other reasonable explanation.

The noises fitted the known history. The giggles and whispering could have been Archibald and his loose women. The screaming and sounds of fire were obviously relics of the actual event. Deciding to change the subject after concluding that the top floor of the house was probably haunted we both vowed to stay away from up there in the future.

I was struck by what an easy person she was to talk to and we were both amazed when we realised that the time was eleven o'clock and although there was no sign of the pub shutting we thought that maybe it was time for us to make our return to the college.

As we got back in the car I was tempted to go for a little kiss but something held me back and I just smiled at her as she clicked her seat belt into position.

'So back to zee prison camp' I chuckled putting on a pseudo German accent.

'I guess unless you'd like to have a little drive around first and see the countryside before we get locked up again. There's no great rush to be back is there?'

'See the countryside? It is absolutely pitch dark out there' I chortled.

'Yes I know but let's just go on enjoying the evening together as once we're back at college there will be lots of others around won't there?'

So I drove for a while not really knowing where I was going but it was pleasant to be with her and she rested her hand on my knee. Soon we came to an area that was wooded on both sides of the road but suddenly the road ran alongside a river which was clearly illuminated by the moonlight that was now shining brightly.

'Gosh that is so beautiful isn't it? Stop for a moment so we can enjoy the view' she suggested speaking quietly and almost immediately I found a place where I could pull the car onto a grass verge. I parked at a diagonal angle so that we had the river view in front of us.

'It's been a lovely evening and now there's this lovely scene to finish'.

'Yes but it doesn't have to be the finish' I replied looking at her.

'Doesn't it?' and she turned to look at me.

Leaning towards her I unbuckled my seat belt so that I could get closer and with a whispered 'May I?' moved my lips towards hers.

'Yes you may. Please' she whispered in reply as she undid her own belt.

The kiss was gentle, soft and delightfully prolonged until we pulled apart and looking into her eyes I said softly 'Thank you'.

'Come here' but this time her lips were much firmer and more demanding as we kissed again, a kiss which became passionate with exploratory forays by our tongues into the other's mouths. We tongued fenced, we pressed, we sighed we became aroused with each other until pulling apart she rested her head on my shoulder as she looked up at me. 'That was good Greg. I'd like to stay here all night with you in this little cocoon of peace and togetherness. Just us completely shut away from the rest of the whole wide world that's outside' and with that she pulled my head to hers and we kissed again and for a very long time.

Whether she was giving me a signal that more of her could be available I don't know but her hand started to run up and down my thigh each time seemingly moving higher and so I slid a hand down her shoulder and across her breasts. She didn't react unfavourably indeed it seemed to me that she moved a little and pressed her chest towards my exploring hand as I eased my mouth away from her and said softly 'Belinda'.

'Umm Greg' she replied as she squeezed the middle of my thigh before laying her head on my shoulder again.

Now I was in a dilemma. The simple fact was that I fancied her like crazy and would like to get her into bed and of course she had that nice big double instead of the little single that I had in my room. However we were in an exposed public place and any further attempts to get at her breasts by undressing her here in the car was unlikely to be acceptable to her in our present location in which the car was brightly illuminated every now and then by the headlights of other vehicles sweeping past. Somehow suggesting that we transferred to the back seat of the car where we might be less on show though didn't seem terribly appropriate and would certainly be pretty undignified wriggling about on there.

Unfortunately she also added to my quandary by saying quietly 'Come on let's go back' but sadly she didn't elaborate on what we might do when we got there!

'Right, back we go then'.

Disentangling ourselves I started the car as we buckled up and soon we were retracing our route back. I still didn't know whether I was soon going to finish up alone in my little bed, or romping round in her double but one possibly hopeful sign was that she again deliberately placed her hand on my leg and slowly stroked the upper part of my thigh as we drove along.

Whether it was this that distracted me I don't know but it didn't take long for me to realise that I'd obviously taken a wrong turning but fortunately having discovered the mistake and turned round we eventually drove into the college car park a little before midnight. After I'd parked I leaned over to kiss her but she put up a hand and gently stopped me.

'No not here Greg. Others might see. It's just not private enough'.

'Ok. Look before we go in I'd like to say I've *really* enjoyed this evening and thanks very much for coming out with me tonight. Perhaps we could do it again while we're both here on this course?'

'Maybe?'

'You don't seem too sure? Haven't you enjoyed tonight?'

'Oh yes I've enjoyed it, in fact I've enjoyed it very much indeed, *all* of it but look it's nearly the witching hour, oops better not use that word in case it summons up more weird things!' she chuckled. 'Any rate it's late and past my bedtime'.

'Hey it is only just past midnight. You're not an early bedder are you?'

'Oh yes I'm a good girl and usually like to be in bed early, so this is definitely late for me'.

'And when you are in bed are you a good girl?' I smirked.

She stared at me with an amused expression flicking around her face before replying 'Sometimes but then again sometimes when I'm in bed I can be a bad girl!' Seeing my surprised expression she added 'Come on Greg it's time to go in' and releasing her safety belt she slid out of the car and stood waiting for me as I pondered what she might have meant? The key question was whether she really was offering me a "come on". Hopefully the next few minutes would tell.

We walked across the gravel and into the main

entrance hallway. There were a few people about but not many although there was a sudden burst of laughter from the bar area as we walked across the huge hallway, her high heels click clacking on the tiled floor as we headed for the stairs.

At the top we paused and looked at each other. Her room was down one of the three corridors while mine was down a different one.

'Err ....' I muttered.

'Thanks for a lovely evening Greg' she replied with a slight smile then after a short pause and before I said anything she turned and set off for her room. I had hoped she might invite me to accompany her but she hadn't so I watched her go then with considerable disappointment turned to my corridor and was soon in my own room where I plonked down in the armchair and thought about the evening before getting up and going into the bathroom. I'd had a pee, and was just about to have quick wash and do my teeth when the phone rang. Quickly I returned to the bedroom and picked it up. 'Hello?'

'You're not very adventurous are you?' came Belinda's soft voice.

'Pardon?'

'Well if you were more adventurous you might find out if I'm going to a good girl tonight' she paused then continued speaking but now much more quietly 'or maybe on the other hand whether I feel like being a bad and really naughty girl tonight. Now what do you say to that?'

'Aah?'

'Yes aah. So do you feel adventurous Greg?'

'Do you know now you mention it then I really think that I do?'

'Well then why don't you come along and see which it is to be?' and with a chuckle she rang off.

Quickly splashing on another little dab of aftershave I walked out of my room, locked the door and was soon outside number 146 where I found her door was not only unlocked but slightly ajar. Pressing it open I peered in.

'Belinda?'

'Yes honey, come on in' and as I looked into her room there she was sitting up in bed holding the duvet cover up to her neck. 'Now Greg shut the door, come over here and see if you can you work out what the answer is?'

Feeling quite lightheaded at the opportunity that seemed to be presenting itself to me but with my feet suddenly leaden I walked slowly over to the bed and sat down beside her.

'Hmm that's better' she said quietly as she ran a hand along my thigh and into the crotch area where she firmly and deliberately pressed her hand against me. 'Now Greg to ensure there is no misunderstanding between us I've decided to give you a few clues in case you're *still* not sure what the answer is? This is the first' and she handed me a condom foil, then as her hands moved to quickly and deftly undo my trouser zip and waist clip and ease the flaps apart she said softly as she slid her fingers inside and started to stroke me through my pants 'and this is the second clue. I hope you're getting the message but just in case you are still in some doubt, here comes your third and last clue' and with a smile she flicked back the duvet cover and slid down onto her back.

Stark naked and with her jet black skin creating a

deep and erotically inviting contrast against the white under sheet she whispered 'Now *if* you've worked out the answer as to whether I'm feeling good or bad, then why don't you take off all those clothes that you're wearing and come and join me?'

***

When I woke in the morning she was still asleep. Glancing at the bedside clock which of course was identical to the one in my room, I saw that it was twenty past eight. That was late for me to wake but then it had been a somewhat energetic time last night after I stripped off and got onto the bed with her. I won't say that she was insatiable but she was certainly pretty inexhaustible and an extremely skilled practioner in the art of making love and I know that in our long sessions together we used two condoms. I'm not sure how many times she orgasmed but it was several judging by the grunts and sighs and squeezing of me that she undertook in the throes of her passion.

As usual I'd woken up with a hard on and it seemed to me that lying beside me was an extremely attractive way of dealing with it so having carefully peeled the duvet cover off her I spent a moment studying her naked shoulders, back, extremely cute bum and lovely long legs before leaning closer to kiss her shoulder. Gently stroking her thigh as I ran my tongue around her ear and along her neck I felt my erection poking against her hip.

She stirred, looked over her shoulder at me, smiled, reached down and grasping my prick gave it a squeeze then muttered 'Umm that feels nice' and twisting to stretch out her neck out she popped a little kiss on my lips.

'Wait there honey' she instructed softly as she rolled out of bed and walked to the bathroom where as she left the door open I heard her peeing followed by the sound of her brushing her teeth then there was the trickling of running water into the basin and some quite loud splashing sounds before she walked back into the bedroom, sat down next to me and leaning down stroked my forehead before kissing me hard. I enjoyed the sensations from her lips to mine, the peppermint taste of her toothpaste but especially the way her tongue straight away probed really deep inside my mouth.

After a little she sat up, smiled then moved a little away from me, opened the bedside drawer and took out a condom which she put on the pillow beside my head after which I lay still enjoying watching her black hands slide around my nipples and pectoral muscles, down my chest, across my belly and finish by grasping my erection where she started rubbing slowly and tenderly.

'Now this is a lovely sight for a girl first thing in the morning isn't it?' she chuckled as her hands teased, squeezed and played with my erection and my balls.

'Oh babe' she murmured as leaning forward and using one hand to sweep her hair out of the way while the other continued to slowly rub me, she popped several kisses up and down the length of me before twisting round to sit beside me.

Reaching forward she carefully rolled the condom onto me and as soon as I was covered lifted herself forward to slowly and carefully lower herself onto me, sighing softly as I slid deep inside her warm and willing intimate entrance.

Leaning down she kissed me and then sighed as I in turn kissed and licked her nipples which already were like hard little peanuts as she began working on me as we started to make love.

Alternating between leaning down to kiss me and stretching upright to press herself down onto me as she moved above me this was a wonderful morning experience but shortly when I saw her bite her lips and groan quietly as she orgasmed then I knew it was time for me to do as well so I warned her that I too was about to climax.

'Squirt away babe' she invited and seconds later I did unleashing my ejaculation into the condom buried inside her body. Pleasingly she continued to move on me until she judged that I'd completely finished then raising an eyebrow asked quietly 'All done?'

'Yes thanks'.

'Good' and with that she stopped moving and just lay forward onto me for a while kissing me softly before sliding off and pulling me into her side where she twisted her head and kissed me firmly and positively on my lips. 'Thanks. That was good babe'.

'Yes it was thank you'.

'So aren't you glad you became adventurous last night?'

'Yes very glad'.

'Yep so am I' then leaning up and resting an elbow on my tummy while she traced a forefinger through my chest hair she asked 'so why didn't you come along by yourself? Why did I have to persuade you?'

'I don't know really. I looked for some signals from

you that you were, err well that is that you might let me take things further but you said goodnight so abruptly at the top of the stairs and walked off that I thought you didn't want me to'.

'Oh well you see I had really expected you to say "hang on can I come to your room" but you didn't and when I looked round you'd gone so I thought I'd better ring you'.

'I'm *very* glad that you did'.

'So am I. Right now go and make me a cup of coffee and whatever you want for yourself' and with a grin she rolled onto her tummy and watched as I got out of bed. Picking up the kettle and going into the bathroom first of all I dropped the used condom down the loo then stood waiting for a few moments until my erection had gone and I could have a pee. Having washed my hands I wrapped a towel around my waist, filled the kettle and went back into the bedroom where I sat on a chair as we chatted while waiting for the kettle to boil. When it did I made two cups of coffee benefitting from the fact that as this was a double room there were two of every utensil unlike the single rooms where there was only one.

I left my cup on the dressing table and carried hers over to where she was lying smiling at me. As I reached the bed and had just put her cup down she reached out and slowly pulled the towel off me, then taking hold of my now flaccid penis said with a glint in her eye 'You're not in any hurry to rush away are you honey?' and she ran her thumb and forefinger which she'd made into a circle up and down my penis.

'Got anything particular in mind?' I laughed quietly,

enjoying watching the contrast between her black fingers and my white cock and balls as she played with me.

''Uh huh definitely, as long as you can get this up again' and with that she wrapped all the fingers of one hand around me and gripping more tightly started to move more quickly. To her obvious delight and my definite relief an erection started and soon had extended to its fullest extent.

'Good now that looks to be just what the doctor, and the lady, ordered' and with a grin she reached into the bedside table drawer, rummaged around, found another condom which she held out to me then wriggled down until she was lying flat on her back as she watched me fit the prophylactic.

As soon as I had she held up her arms and invited me to climb on top of her and being a gentleman then I thought it would have been most impolite to refuse as I felt her legs wrap themselves around me!

***

Later as we were lying cuddled together, stroking and peck kissing each other I asked 'Do you remember what time they serve breakfast to on Sundays? I know it is eight thirty Monday to Saturday but on our one day off I assume it will be later'.

With a quick look at the clock she replied 'Ten I think so we've got thirty five minutes. Can't think where all the time has gone since we woke up! Right up you get. I need a shower. See you later eh?' and with a quick kiss on my lips she was out of bed. Picking up my clothes from the chair where I'd chucked them after my frantic stripping off last night she threw them at me with a grin and said 'Right off you go' and turning away walked into the bathroom giving me a last enjoyable glance of the back view of her pert and naked black buttocks.

I pulled on my trousers, shirt and shoes and was soon skulking along her corridor, down mine and back into my own room where I undressed, showered and at ten to ten I walked into the dining room where there were half a dozen or so others who by the look of it had almost finished eating. I helped myself from the remains of the hot breakfast buffet and sat down on my own and it was almost exactly ten when she walked in, smiled at me, helped herself to some cereals and fruit and then to my surprise didn't join me but went and sat down next to another man who looked to be of about my age but a little taller and blonde haired, whereas I am dark haired.

Odd I thought as somehow I'd sort of assumed that Belinda and I would spend the day together but it seemed as if she was deliberately ignoring me. Perhaps she didn't want to be seen to be with me as probably others had seen us go out last night and indeed possibly return after our meal.

I was still pondering this when Richard another member of our course but who'd been in a different syndicate plonked down next to me with a couple of croissants, a bread roll, some jam and a cup of coffee.

'Morning Greg. God I feel a bit rough this morning. Comes of sitting up till gone one o'clock supping pints I suppose' he laughed then winced.

'Surely the bar wasn't open till that time?'

'No but a couple of guys and me, well we kind of lined up a few before they shut at eleven'.

'A few?' I laughed.

'Err well four pints each to be exact, I think' he laughed again. 'Seemed a good idea at the time but when I woke up this morning a little while ago I'm not so sure. Bloody good job we haven't got any classes today as I'm not sure me and my thumping headache could quite cope with the intricacies of the finer points of management!' he laughed then immediately winced before taking a slow and thoughtful sip of his coffee.

We started to chat about what we each thought of the first week and I didn't see Belinda leave but when I finished my second cup of coffee and stood up to go leaving Richard still quietly nursing his hangover I saw that she wasn't in the dining room. I wandered into one of the lounges but she wasn't there nor was she in any of the other downstairs rooms.

Going to the phone on the unmanned reception desk I dialled her room and moments later she answered.

'Oh hi there, it's Greg. I wondered if you'd like to spend time together today? Maybe go for a walk in the grounds or have a swim or perhaps play a game of badminton or squash?'

'No thanks'.

'Oh'.

'Was there anything else?'

'Err well no. I just thought ....'

'Well don't! Right see you later then' and she rang off.

Blimey! What a change. Less than an hour ago she'd had her naked arms and legs wrapped around me happily enjoying all sorts of intimate sexual fun things together, but now she was as cold as ice and clearly giving me the elbow!

So I went for a swim by myself, then had a walk through the grounds which really were quite delightful before returning where I settled down in the lounge with the newspapers and started to work my way through several different titles enjoying comparing the diverse approach to an identical news item taken by each paper depending on whether they were to the left or right of the political spectrum.

For lunch I just had some soup and a mixed salad and I was about half way through eating when Belinda came in, smiled at me then helped herself to some salad but went and sat at a different table and engaged in conversation with some other people.

A definite brush off! Quite extraordinary!

I spent a couple of hours dozing on my bed in my own room during the afternoon catching up on some sleep but at four still feeling a bit jaded I went and had another swim, then afterwards changed and was in our lecture room for the five o'clock restart.

Belinda was already been in the room when I walked in so I went over and sat next to her as we had the previous week.

'Hi there everything ok?' I asked quietly.

'Yes fine thanks'.

'Oh only ......'

I was interrupted by Tony walking in and saying briskly to the room in general 'Hello there everyone. Well have you enjoyed your free time? I hope so because you aren't going to have any free time this week! Not a single second!' and he laughed.

'Right now to get us back into work mode I want each of you to tell me the three most important things that you learnt here last week. So someone start us off. Shout out your three and I'll put them on the board here then we'll add everyone else's points' and standing by an easel holding large sheets of white paper and with a black marker pen he looked expectantly at the class.

Belinda completely ignored me for the two hour session as we called out our suggestions which were gradually built up into an interesting and impressive list in which surprisingly although there was some variation seemed to largely focus onto the same seven or eight points that most of us mentioned and it was those that the whole class debated with Tony.

As we left the room a little before seven clutching the brief for our personal evening project I headed for the bar and supper where I intended to try and button hole Belinda but she'd got into conversation with someone else as she walked out and although I went to the bar she didn't. After the gong sounded for dinner I was already seated when she came into the room but ignoring my facial plea and nod of the head for her to join me, instead she went and sat at the opposite end of the table and immediately got into conversation with the people around her there.

She seemed to eat her meal rather quickly and by the time I'd finished she'd left the room. I guessed she was in her own room so when I'd also finished I went upstairs and knocked on the door of 146.

'Yes?' she asked when she opened the door.

'Look have I upset you or something?'

'No why?'

'Well you seem to be ignoring me. I mean I can't understand it as last night and earlier this morning .....'

'Last night and earlier this morning, were last night and earlier this morning. Were. Past tense. They're not now'.

'No I realise that but ......'

'Look Greg. I'll spell it out for you if you like as you seem a bit slow on the uptake. I enjoyed your company, the meal at the pub was enjoyable and our time in bed last night and again this morning was terrific. You were good to be with, the sex was great and I've had a really fun time with you. But that is all it was. Fun. Nothing serious. I have no regrets but it is *over*. I am not looking for any sort of relationship or affair while I am here with you or anyone. A one nighter is fine and exactly what I wanted but that's all it was. Alright?'

'So you don't want to go out again or have ......'

'No Greg babe' and she sighed somewhat theatrically 'I don't want to go out with you or have sex with you again. Look frankly there are plenty of other men here and I quite fancy one or two of them and who knows? Maybe I'll get it together with someone else but if I do it will again be just for another one night stand. Got it?'

'Yes got it' I said distinctly crestfallen.

'Hey cheer up. There are a few ladies here that might like a good shag to take their mind off their study projects! Try your luck with one of them eh?'

'I don't really want ......'

'Look stop it. I've told you what the position is regarding you and me. Now would you go please and let me get on with my work?' and stepping back she quietly but firmly closed the door in my face.

I walked slowly and I have to admit rather sadly back to my own room and as I sat down at the desk unit and started to look at the evening study project I muttered aloud 'Well well well. Fun, frolics, fucked, finished and all in the space of a few hours'.

What made it all the more upsetting was that this was the first time I'd ever slept with a black woman and I have to say I'd enjoyed the experience.

Apart from a quick one night fling with a very attractive young lady whose parents were originally from Pakistan, then all my previous conquests had been traditional Anglo Saxon white. Admittedly of various shapes, sizes, backgrounds, accents, interests, jobs and ages although to be fair most had been in their twenties or early thirties, except one lady who'd I'd pulled one night when I'd had a lot more to drink than was advisable when nookie hunting.

I'd certainly got a shock when I woke up alongside her next morning and realised that probably the reason she'd been so good at the sex stuff was that she'd had plenty of years to practice because when we were sitting in her kitchen having tea and toast, there sitting on her dresser unit were several birthday cards congratulating her on reaching her fiftieth!

In my defence I have to say that she didn't look that old even then in the cold light of morning! Nevertheless it was a significant jolt to the system!

CHAPTER 4

As the tutors had warned the second week's work proved to be more difficult, more demanding and requiring much more thought than had week one. All twelve of us were attending the classes in the same main lecture room of course but as Tony had said the syndicates were completely different and neither Peter, Raymond nor Belinda were in my new grouping which now comprised a middle aged lady called Zoe and two men, Keith who'd seemed a bit morose from what I seen of him from time to time last week and Jason who'd suffered Belinda's sharp put down at the table when he'd tried to chat her up.

Keith proved to be a bit domineering and seemed to like to hog conversations in our syndicate discussions and several times Jason, Zoe or I had to insist that he stopped talking or pontificating and listened to other people's ideas. By Tuesday evening frankly the three others of us had simply had enough of him and matters came to a head that evening with a right royal row resulting in him stomping off, leaving the others of us to finish the project.

When we had completed the work we all went to the bar and mutually drowned our annoyance with him and it gave me the opportunity to learn a little more about my fellow syndicate members.

Jason was Sales manager for a company making and selling garden equipment ranging from hoses to wooden benches. He was apparently earmarked to be promoted sometime in the next year or so and was being prepared for this by being sent on this course. He was married with two young children. A keen squash player he seemed to be an all round good chap in spite of trying and failing to chat up Belinda.

Zoe was attractive and as I guessed her age at around forty then she was several years older than me. Ten to be precise. Divorced but now in a new relationship although I gathered from one or two things that she let slip that maybe she wasn't overly happy with her new man with whom she'd been living for about a year.

None of us knew much about Keith except that he was a Director in a business which made various sorts of metal castings and was here to learn about modern management techniques and procedures although as Zoe said quietly to me on one occasion the chances of that fat bigot learning anything different from his own hard held views and beliefs was going to be very limited.

Next morning Keith refused to be part of the presentation that we were giving and insisted on presenting his own minority report first which was entirely different from what we were going to explain and I have to say also quite at odds with the presentation already given by the first group to present that morning.

Janet handled the disruption well though as after listening to Keith she said 'Well it's not the first time we've had a minority report following a syndicate bust up here and I doubt whether it will be the last. You certainly have some interesting if somewhat forthright views Keith but I am not sure that they are suited to present day modern management which no longer works on the "mushroom management" philosophy'.

Turning to the other eleven course members in class she smiled as she said 'For those that are not familiar with "mushroom management" it is basically just as you do when growing mushrooms. Keep everyone in the dark but every now and then open the door and tip a great load of shit over everything and everyone then shut the door and revert to keeping everything in the dark again!'

There was an instant burst of laughter from eleven people while Keith scowled and responded irritably 'You can all mock. I don't hold with all this "we're in it together" stuff. Workers do best if directed and controlled by management and are only told the minimum. Need to know basis. Worked in wartime. Works now' and he stuck his chin out aggressively.

'The war and by that I assume you mean the second world war, finished sixty five years ago Keith. Don't you think that it might be worth considering a new approach to managing your people and while we're at it note that I call them people not workers like you do?'

While he struggled to find a reply she smiled sweetly and said 'So thanks for your presentation Keith but can I now suggest you take a seat while the other three members of the syndicate come and present their thoughts' and with her charm and experience she had defused a potentially tricky and disruptive moment.

Zoe and I made the presentation between us with Jason nodding agreement and adding a couple of points that we forgot.

So the week went on. The work veered between difficult, very difficult, interesting, mind twistingly complicated and occasionally boring, but overall although it was hard and we in our syndicate were working till nearly midnight every night with most evenings Keith supporting and helping although sometimes he'd wander off to the bar and not take any further part in our discussions, I was thoroughly enjoying the learning process and realised how much new material I was absorbing which would undoubtedly stand me in excellent stead for the future.

Belinda continued to ignore me apart from an occasional smile or a passing word although on Friday morning at coffee break she sidled up to me.

'Hi Greg. So how's your new syndicate? That Keith seems an awkward customer?'

'Yes he can be but Jason and Zoe are great'.

'Umm Zoe. Now she's divorced and from what she said to me when we were chatting the other day then she's not overly happy with her new man is she? That probably means she's frustrated and frustrated women get horny so although she's got a good few years on you why don't you see if you can't solve that little problem for her with what you've got tucked away inside those pants of yours eh?' and her smile was pure wickedness.

'I don't think she's the slightest bit interested in a quick leg over while she's here'.

'You might be surprised'.

'Talking about leg overs is there any chance that we ....'

'No there isn't. Absolutely none at all. I have already sorted out my next man and this weekend he's going to find all his birthdays have come at once' and with a wink and a thoroughly dirty chuckle she sashayed away from me leaving me to wonder who the lucky, or maybe unlucky guy was that she'd got in her sights?

Come the weekend again we didn't get Saturday off and indeed it was a full work day up right up to seven o'clock but then like last week there wasn't any Saturday evening project work and Sunday was again free. Several people went out for the evening but somehow I didn't feel like doing so and when I wandered into the dining room I made up a small table with Zoe and Jason together with Nick another member of our course plus Christine and Susan who were from an entirely different course but seemed quite friendly with Zoe.

It was a pleasant enough evening but there was no sign of Belinda. She hadn't been in to dinner and was nowhere around in the bar or lounges.

Jason and I had a couple of games of snooker and then had a fun time teaching Zoe and Susan to play before Christine and I had a game of darts at which she beat me hands down. I only discovered afterwards that she was a keen member of her local pub's darts team and played regularly in matches against other pubs and clubs. No wonder she clobbered me!

As the bar closed at eleven I topped up my pint and ordered in another and then settled down to play a game of chess with Keith who'd appeared and seemed to want to be friendly. Now I am a reasonably good at chess having been taught by my dad who was an excellent player but I soon found out that Keith was a real hot shot at the game and far too good for me. I lost two games and was about to call it a day when I spotted Belinda and another chap not from our course going past the door from the bar into the hallway obviously having been out together for the evening. Quickly I excused myself and hurried into the hall in time to see them reach the top of the stairs and without any hesitation they held hands and walked straight down the corridor that led to her room. Oh well she'd obviously succeeded in her plan and now all that was left for me to do was to wonder if the guy was going to enjoy his multi birthday session!

I returned to Keith and the chess but in a couple of further moves I was checkmated so conceding defeat I went to bed where I read a novel for a while then turned out the light and after a short period of tossing and turning was soon asleep although just before I woke up next morning I dreamed that I'd invited Zoe into my room and seduced her. It was quite vivid and as a result my usual morning wake up hard on seemed stronger than usual. The effect of licentious thoughts about Zoe I guessed as I got into the shower.

This morning being Sunday as we had no classes or work to do and with the day free until five o'clock I didn't rush to get up. However when I had and was eating my breakfast in the dining room I was interested to see Belinda walk in on her own, smile at me, help herself to cereals and fruit and then surprise surprise, she came and sat down next to me.

'Good morning' she beamed. 'Did you have a good evening?'

'Yeah it was ok. I played some snooker and darts, had a few beers, got soundly beaten at chess, chatted a bit then went to bed and read for a while. And you?'

'Uh huh. Harvey and I went out and had a Chinese then we came back here and he found out just what an extremely horny naughty black girl could do for him' she giggled quietly.

'And have you dumped him already this morning?'

'No'.

'No?'

'No. I dumped him last night. I can put up with a

guy who's not brilliant in bed but I can't be doing with one who can only get it up once! So when we'd done the dirty deed last night and suddenly discovering that was the limit of his ability in spite of several things I tried to help which usually work with men who are having, err shall we say "getting it up again problems". But sadly none of them seemed to succeed for him so I suggested he went back to his own room which like a good fellow he did'.

'Look as you well know I can get it up more than once so if you'd like ....'

'No Greg. I told you, one night stands is all I want. Besides there is a new intake of candidates today for a couple of the other courses so there's bound to be a nice man who would like to enjoy the benefits of my brilliant mind, my witty charm, my naked body' and leaning close to me and dropping her voice to a mere whisper she added 'and my dirty mind' then patting my hand she smiled as she leant back in her chair but moments later she again leant close to my ear and very quietly 'So did you get it on with Zoe?'

'No and I didn't try'.

'Idiot' she grinned. 'Listen I'm going to have a swim later this morning, say around eleven. Fancy doing a few lengths with me? Give you a chance to have another leer at my body won't it?'

The day dragged by. I did swim with her and at one point when we were both at the deep end the cheeky little minx quickly pulled her bikini top down and briefly exposed her breasts to me then with a little smirk covered them up again.

I did play some more snooker. I did go for a walk.

I did have a rest on my bed. I did have a quick look at some notes from yesterday's work and on an impulse I did get up to go and have a wander around up on the second floor.

Why I don't know? I just did but the moment that I started walking along the corridor which not only seemed, but actually was dingier and darker than those on the first floor, then I felt something like a shroud of malevolence envelope me. It almost seemed clammy and I got the feeling that someone or something was following me but I carried on until I came to my old room 209.

Gingerly I pushed open the door which was unlocked and walked inside. It was exactly as I remembered and indeed virtually identical to the room I now occupied. The bed had been made, there were clean towels hanging on the rail by the wardrobe and tray had been replenished with tea and coffee and sachets of powdered milk and as I looked around I heard the door click shut.

Quickly I walked to it and twisted the handle. It opened and I couldn't help but give an involuntary sigh of relief as I turned back into the room and walked over to the bed where I lay down and closed my eyes.

For a moment I felt calm and at peace but then it started exactly as before. The giggles, the whispers, the footsteps and suddenly the screaming and acrid smell of burning accompanied by the sound of wood crackling like it does in a fire.

That was it. I wanted out and right now!

Realising I shouldn't have come back here I jumped up and went to the door which again for some reason had shut but this time it wouldn't open. Much as I twisted and tugged the door remained stubbornly shut. The screams got louder and they were now interspersed with sounds of cackling female laughter. I ran to the window to see if I could open that but it too was shut. Locked and there was no key to be seen to release the stout locking catch.

'Think logically' I said to myself trying to ignore the cacophony going on around me and taking hold of the door I tried with all my might to twist the handle. Still it wouldn't budge. The smell of smoke was getting stronger. In a rage I kicked the damn thing then leaning against the wall to the side of the door I slid to the floor squatting on my haunches with my eyes shut, head down and my hands over my ears.

All of a sudden as abruptly as they'd started, the noises stopped. I cocked my head to one side and gingerly took my hands away from covering my ears. I listened intently. Nothing. No sound at all. Also no burning smell. I stood looking warily around me. Still I was alone and in silence. Cautiously I tried the door handle. It turned straight away and the door opened immediately to my pull.

As quickly as I could I rushed through that door, slammed it closed behind me and although I am ashamed to admit it I ran down the corridor to the end where it emerged at the top of the second staircase. Forcing myself to do so I turned round and looked back along the passageway down which I'd just run. There was nothing to be seen but as I turned back to face the stairs I thought I might have heard a sound of laughter.

I was down that top flight like a shot and hurried until I was in my own room where I threw myself on the bed and thought about what had happened. I even pinched myself to see if I'd been dreaming. I lay there trying to come up with some rationale explanation but couldn't. However one thing I did decide was that I was never going up to the top floor again. Ever!

***

The third week's work was again tough and demanding. The problems posed by the various projects became more complex and not only increasingly difficult but seemed to offer several possible solutions which caused many heated debates in the class course group as a whole as well as within our syndicate discussions which after another Monday morning's reshuffle of syndicate members now consisted of Zoe and me from the week 2 grouping with the addition of Richard who worked for a pharmaceutical company in their research department and was making the transition from complex laboratory management work to senior general management and seemed an affable sort of chap. The fourth member was Maggie a lady who was probably around Zoe's age. She worked for British Telecom and I'd chatted to her on several occasions in the bar during the first two weeks and found her easy going, quite laid-back, straightforward and with a nice sense of humour.

We were a good team and worked well together which was good as not only were we often still hard at it until midnight or on one occasion till just after one am, but Tony had announced that we'd be in these syndicate groups for the whole of weeks three and four and that there would be no further changes.

I saw Belinda occasionally at break and meal times and although on a couple of occasions I tried to persuade her to let me go to bed with her again, each time she refused. She was quite nice about it but utterly adamant and I noticed that she was making up to a couple of blokes on another course I knew she was going to definitely pursue her one night only per man approach. In this quest she obviously succeeded as on the Friday night of week three when our syndicate finished work around eight thirty as we trooped into the bar for a well earned drink, I saw Belinda walking out of the hallway with a man who I recognised as having been on a one week course that finished that day. Normally people can't wait to get away at the end of the incarceration on the college to get back to normality but I learnt later that she'd got her hooks into him and persuaded him to hang around and wait until she was free that evening.

From the look on his face next morning it seemed that the wait had obviously been worthwhile! I think he probably returned to wherever he came from a very happy man!

We all again worked throughout Saturday but to my amazement Belinda came into dinner beside Keith and sat with him, chatting and laughing throughout their meal after which they went to the bar where the two of them got rather touchy feely.

After eating I too went to the bar and settled down to a discussion with Jason, Maggie and Richard on the latest business challenge that we'd all been given to read before starting work again on Sunday evening at five and I enjoyed the discussion and friendly arguments that ensued about the best way to handle the project.

This was in fact an important part of the whole four week course learning method as it wasn't just what we learnt in the classroom from the various tutors and teachers, or what we worked out together in the syndicate groups, nor indeed our own individual study work but also what we learnt from these types of informal debate and discussions.

At some stage I left to have a quick pee and when I came back Belinda and Keith had both left and as neither reappeared for the rest of the evening then it was a pretty good indication that the two of them were hard at it in either his single bedroom but more likely in her larger double bed.

On Sunday morning I went for a run, swam, played snooker with some of the others and enjoyed relaxing reading the Sunday papers and it wasn't until lunch time that she made an appearance in the bar. I walked over and offered to buy her a drink which she accepted and asked for a glass of red wine and after I'd got it and sat down with her in a corner I grinned, raised my beer glass and said 'Cheers. Here's to sex'.

She grinned and replied 'Yes to sex, and lots of it'.

'Keith?' I queried raising an eyebrow.

'Ooh I couldn't possibly say' she giggled quietly then seeing my quizzical look leaned forward and speaking in a low voice added 'well alright then yes, and he's quite a stud for an older man!'

'You are incorrigible. He's married and got a couple of kids you know'.

'Well I shan't tell his wife and I very much doubt that he will either so where's the harm eh? Any rate you watch as I bet he's not nearly so grumpy this week now that I've cheered him up!'

Seeing my disapproving expression she said 'Oh come on Greg stop being such a prude. Without a man I get horny so I need a man to deal with that problem. In any case I don't remember you complaining when we got it together and correct me if I'm wrong but haven't you tried several times since we did to persuade me to sleep with you again?'

'Well yes but .....'

'But nothing. You're just jealous. Now the gong's sounded and I'm hungry so shall we go in to lunch together?'

We did and sat next to each other and chatted about all sorts of inconsequential things, the work, what the final week might hold and our mutual thoughts on our personal study project what we were all going to discuss in class at five that afternoon.

It was as we were having dessert that Keith came in, waved at Belinda and me, selected some soup and a plate of salad for his meal and then took a place at a table to the side of the room where he sat with his back to the wall. As Belinda and I left he was still eating, but she left me and went round to his side of the table where he was now the only person sitting and said hello. He didn't notice that I saw that while returning her greeting he also slid his hand up her thigh and across her buttocks where he paused and squeezed at which she grinned, wagged her finger and eased herself away from him.

He returned her grin and then she left him and rejoined me to walk together to the room for coffee, after which I said that I was committed to playing in a darts match at three while she told me that she was going to have a lie down and rest for a while as it had been a rather energetic night!

'We could make it an energetic afternoon if you like?' I suggested.

'Thought you were playing darts?'

'Yes I am but I'm sure someone else could take my place'.

'Oh no doubt, but I'd hate to deprive your team of your throwing skills so I think we'll go our separate ways shall we? Besides after I've caught up on a little beauty sleep I need to have a look at our study project as I haven't done anything about it yet'.

***

Our final week started on that Sunday evening with a class discussion about the study project and it was soon clear that many of us, including me, had missed several of the more subtle points buried away within the papers that we'd been given. It was a good lesson to us all I guess but one which I certainly took to heart and that was to ensure that you've fully understood *all* of the elements of a business problem before leaping to solutions and haven't just focussed on what seemed to be the most obvious matters facing you

On Monday afternoon we were scheduled to have a lecture from an American called Professor Henderson. Tony our course tutor had said during the morning, admittedly with a smile as well as a twinkle in his eye that we'd find the Professor an interesting character and probably not what we expected.

He was right because when we returned from lunch standing at the front of the lecture room chatting to Tony was a woman in her late thirties. She was wearing a surprisingly short pale pink pleated skirt matched with a white blouse, had long blonde hair and was simply stunning. I glanced around the room and all the other men were, like me, transfixed by her stunningly good looks.

'Right as everyone is now back from lunch I'd like to introduce you to Professor Henderson who if nothing else proves two things. Firstly that university professors don't all have to be miserable grumpy old men wearing scruffy clothes and reeking of pipe tobacco and secondly that extremely attractive women don't just have to go into the glamour profession to get recognition in their chosen field. So enjoy your afternoon and I'll see you later' and with that he left us.

As soon as he'd gone our vision of loveliness hitched herself up onto the small table at the front of the room, carefully crossed her legs, demurely pulled her skirt hem down as far as it would go which still left a long expanse of delightful leg exposed and smiled at us.

'Hi everyone' and we all immediately delighted in her soft mid-western American accent. 'As Tony said I am Professor Henderson but I'd be really happy for you to call me Loretta. Now this afternoon we're gonna be looking at different strategic planning tools and techniques and I'd advise you to listen real well as your next big syndicate project which I believe runs from tonight through Tuesday is all around planning and the dire effects on businesses who didn't do it very well'.

Shortly she slid carefully off the table and lectured us while walking around at the front of the room and proved that as well as being lovely she was a very interesting and amusing speaker with an amazingly quick mind but who had a real skill in listening to questions and points made by us and then incorporating the answer not only into real life examples but also some of the course work which we'd undertaken in the time that we'd been studying at the college.

When she called time for a mid afternoon break for coffee, tea or soft drink I could hardly believe that an hour and a half had gone by, a feeling that was shared by everyone else on the course including both Maggie and Zoe who weren't catty about Loretta's appearance but fascinated by her skill, knowledge and great presentation style.

Belinda though sidled up to me as we were starting to make our way back into the lecture hall and said quietly 'Hey Greg for this afternoon's session you and the other guys might do better if you put your tongues back in your mouths and stopped drooling' then with a chuckle she patted me on the bottom and walked beside me into the lecture room.

'Ok guys and girls I am going to divide you into two groups' and Loretta pointed her arm to separate the room into two. You to the left can stay in here. You to the right can go to one of the syndicate rooms. I believe Ash has been put aside for your use this afternoon. Here is what I want you to work on' and she walked round the room handing out a folder containing several papers. Returning to the front of the room when she'd finished handing out the papers she spoke again.

'Spend a little time reading the brief independently, before discussing it as a group, then start to address the issues but I warn you that they are more multifaceted than you might imagine at first read through, so don't jump to your assumptions too quickly. Ask yourselves "Have I *really* thought this through *completely and thoroughly?*" before you come to your final conclusions.

You've got from now until nine o'clock this evening at which point I want you all back in here and each group will make a presentation (which she pronounced in the American way as preezentation) of ten minutes then we'll have a class discussion and with luck we'll get through just before the bar shuts. Oh yes by the way. For whoever it is of you that gets there first then make a note will you that mine is a glass of chilled white wine!' and with a delightful smile she turned away signalling that our work was now to start.

Eventually we made it to the bar at twenty minutes to eleven. It was Jason who bought Loretta her wine and I have to admit that my reason for pushing through the small crowd around her by the bar wasn't just because I had a question related to the project but also I really wanted to get up close to her as she was simply stunning.

Later when I went to bed my mind wasn't just spinning from everything that we'd learnt today but also because Loretta was so disturbingly attractive and it took me some while to go off to sleep.

Tuesday morning was spent in the main lecture room with Tony and Janet reprising the main points from the many projects, challenges, discussions and issues that we'd handled during the previous three and a half weeks, then after lunch we were briefed on the big project to which all the work of the preceding weeks had been leading.

Dauntingly it was going to take us the rest of that afternoon and evening late into the night; all of Wednesday until very late at night and the early part of Thursday morning. At that point we had to have detailed thirty minute presentations finished, with copies made for all the other course members plus Tony and Janet and be ready to physically make the half hour presentation to the whole group from ten o'clock on that Thursday. The plan was that the three half hour presentations together with half hour class discussion of each of them would fill Thursday from ten until lunch time.

Then the afternoon would be a review in class by the whole group of the project, the presentations, the different thoughts and ideas put forward and the overall learning that we experienced from it.

To our amazement and delight we were also told that there would be no course or project work on that coming Thursday evening as that was reserved for a gala dinner for us and that sounded as though it was going to be a welcome relief after what appeared to be stacking up like an horrendous couple of days. Finally Friday morning would be a review of the whole four week course and we'd be free to leave after lunch on that day.

As we were released to get on with the assignment our little collective group of four had a quick meeting at the back of the main lecture room where we rapidly agreed that we should all go separately somewhere alone and study the brief, make notes and then reconvene in an hour to discuss, plan and agree a common approach for the way forward.

So I went to my room, sat at the little desk, laid out the many different documents and papers that we'd been given and quickly paged through them, noting that there were several graphs, sub-briefs, financial schedules and complex details about the fictitious business called Many Challenges Limited which had all these problems and issues that we were to study and solve.

The plan was that the four of us all gathered together again at four thirty for a general discussion on our thoughts and initial points that had struck us from our quick first individual look at the issue. For this we found that we'd been allocated a syndicate room called Maple on the ground floor of the old house. This was the first time that had happened as all our previous work in syndicate rooms had been in rooms located in the new block but there were some rooms still used in the old house and this is where we were going to be for much of the next couple of days.

These syndicate rooms in the old house were slightly smaller, not air conditioned and being wood panel lined were darker than those in the purpose built new block but as Richard said, at least we were nearer the bar for when we felt in need of sustenance and refreshment!

However I also remembered that it had been in that particular small room during the first week when I'd tried to find somewhere away from the top floor to study quietly, that I'd thought I had felt a presence of something odd. Never mind I mused. That was probably all because both Belinda and I were still het up about the second floor strange noises and goings-on, and as I'd not actually seen or heard anything in that room called Maple I told myself to forget it and smilingly agreed with the suggestion that we'd all meet there later in the afternoon.

As well as working well Zoe, Maggie, Richard and I also all got on well and we were looking forward to this challenge that had been set us and also were determined to ensure that we won the competition for the best result as Janet had surprisingly announced that in addition to the prizes that right at the start of the course they'd said could be won, there was a special additional prize for the group of four achieving the best result with this long project.

We duly met at four thirty and agreed that this was going to be a really difficult challenge and so it proved to be. It was hard work and for a long time we didn't seem to be making any real progress on solving the issues, questions and problems that we'd been set and by the time the dinner gong rang we were still unclear as to the right way forward. I was immersed in some financial schedules so I told the others that I'd catch them up in a few minutes as I just wanted to complete the set of numbers on which I was working.

Moments later I was alone in the room although surrounded by sheets of paper pinned to the board at the front, stuck to the wall, piles of computer print outs and lots of rough notes but I was starting to see the answer to the particular part of the overall project that I was handling as we'd divided our assignment into a number of sections and allocated those amongst ourselves. Some we were going to be working on alone, others in twos and some we'd agreed that the whole team of four would handle. It was an effective way of breaking the complex task down into manageable sized pieces.

Suddenly what I was working on became clear and quickly making a final couple of notes I leaned back almost ready to get up and go to eat. I closed my eyes and relaxed for a few minutes after which as I sat upright and opened my eyes again I saw him. The other man in the room.

'Alone then?' he said.

I'd not heard anyone come in and he certainly wasn't part of our syndicate team. Nor was he part of either of the other two syndicate groups. I'd also not seen him as a lecturer in our classes; neither had I spotted him as a possible member of any of the other groups or courses at the college; and for some reason I didn't think he was a tutor or college adviser. I looked at him more closely.

I wasn't sure what exactly he was wearing but it seemed to be that everything that he had on was black. Although seated he gave an impression that when standing he would be tall. His face was pale, sallow even but it was his eyes that transfixed me as they were red. Bright red.

'Who are you?' I queried.

'I'm here to help you'.

Something immediately made me feel distinctly uneasy so shaking my head I stood, smiled and moved quickly to the door where I turned to him. He was sitting exactly where he'd been moments before when I got up.

'I'm going to eat' I announced as I opened the door and walked out into the corridor which led to the main hallway. I shut the door then on an impulse quickly opened it again and looked inside the room.

Nothing. No-one was there. No man in a black suit with strange eyes.

Giving an involuntary shiver I hurried to the dining room where my three colleagues waved at me and pointed to a spare space so I joined them.

'Ok?' asked Maggie. 'Get your numbers done? Do they make sense?'

'Yes and .....'

'And?'

Suddenly I decided not to say anything about what

I'd seen so I replied 'Oh yes, err and I think that there is a clue to cracking the part of the project with the employee issues if we look at how many are short serving people. What the company lacks is experience in depth of really long serving experienced people'.

I paused to give my order to the waitress who was hovering beside me and then Maggie leaned across the table to Richard and said 'Rich, Greg's got an interesting point regarding length of service of the employees?'

'Really. You mean there are too many old timers there?'

'No quite the reverse' I corrected. 'Look that particular factory in the Group is a specialist producer of high quality premium priced cakes and yet they've let most of the long serving experienced people go and replaced them with cheaper newly recruited employees, many of who don't speak English, don't know the British tradition of eating cake, probably have never eaten one themselves and don't have the craft skills that are needed to make and crucially decorate these pricey cakes'.

He looked at me, nodded, clicked his fingers and smiling said 'Hey I think you've got something there. Well done. Now if that's the key to that factory in this fictitious group that we're going to be putting right, then now we need to find the solution to the problems in the other three factories and their product ranges'.

Maggie nodded and Zoe grinned as adding her approval to my idea she also enlarged her comment by saying 'And it seems to me that they are not properly accounting for all the wastage at factory number Two. I can't find any reference to it in the accounts and yet the narrative part of the brief stressed that it is a wasteful process with high levels of discarded or spoilt product; much unused material which is thrown away and a great deal of re-working of some finished products. Yet none of that is in the figures and so that might go part way to explaining why they are not making as much money as they thought they should'.

We all nodded wisely as it was important to encourage each other and the point that Zoe had identified could be an important part of solving some of the profitability issues raised in the task.

During the meal we chatted generally about the project as we ate and then when we'd all finished we went to the coffee room, collected mugs which we filled and then by mutual consent went back to Maple room where as I was in the lead of our little phalanx I somewhat gingerly pushed the door open and peered inside.

Nothing. No strange man.

'Come on you're holding up the experts getting to work' chuckled Maggie as she pressed me from behind and soon all four of us were in the room where we settled down to work again. From time to time I glanced up or around the room but there was only the four of us. During the evening Richard went to the bar and returned with a tray on which were two pint glasses brimming with beer one for him and the other for me, a bottle of lager for Maggie and a Coke for Zoe.

I took my turn and did another bar run just before eleven and returned with top-ups for us all and we worked on our challenge until around half past midnight when first Zoe immediately supported by Maggie said they'd had enough for the night and that they were going to bed and would see Richard and I at breakfast.

As she gathered up her things I took the opportunity to study Maggie and decided that she was actually quite attractive. In fact the more I looked the more I thought she was quite fanciable. Early to mid forties and always smartly dressed but as she leaned down to pick up her handbag her blouse gaped open revealing that beneath was a truly impressive pair of breasts closeted within a white lacy bra. Behave I told myself. You're getting horny from being closeted here and Belinda cutting off supplies of sexual fun after what had been a promising start with her!

Richard and I worked on until a little after one Richard stood up, yawned, said his brain was going round and round in circles and that he too was going to call it a day for now and that he'd see me in the morning.

Surprisingly I didn't feel particularly tired and as there was a particular piece of work which I'd been allocated in our share out of tasks that I had almost completed so I thought I'd work on it for a little while to try and finish it tonight then I could start fresh on another part of the project tomorrow morning.

I'm not sure how long I was working alone in that room before I went to bed but suddenly a voice said 'Alone again then?'

There he was sitting opposite me exactly as before.

'Look who the hell are you?' I demanded quietly.

'Hell? Aah yes now there's an interesting concept?'

'What do you mean?'

'Shall we have some more light?'

'More light? We've got plenty of light from the main overhead lamp above us which is quite bright enough for me thanks?'

'No I mean candle light'.

'Candle light?' I asked incredulously.

The funny thing was I didn't see him move and yet suddenly he was no longer sitting at the table but standing beside the old mantelpiece holding two black candles.

'Look I don't know who you are or what you want but I don't think we want candles lit here. In any case I'm going to bed right now' and standing I left the work at which I'd been toiling and moved towards the door which I opened and looked back into the room. He stared at me with those dull red eyes which seemed to get brighter like an electric hot plate and glow bright red. I couldn't help a little tremble run through me as I slammed the door shut and walked quickly through the old building, up the stairs and into my room which I locked.

***

I lay in bed for a while thinking about the vision, or apparition that I'd seen and decided that I was obviously more tired than I thought I was and as a result my mind had been playing tricks on me, but gradually my worries about it faded and were replaced by questions about the project and soon I was asleep. I don't know whether it was a dream or if in fact I really did wake up but at some stage in the night when it was still dark I saw those red eyes again glowing ever brighter and staring at me.

At breakfast I chatted to Richard, Maggie and Zoe and also exchanged a bit of banter with some of the members of the other two syndicates about how well we were doing as a team and how they were bound to lose the competition amongst the three groups of us.

I grinned at Belinda as she was looking rather grumpy

and then Richard, Zoe, Maggie and I were back in our syndicate room working on the project. We toiled away all day only really breaking from time to time to collect mugs of coffee, go and have some lunch, tea and coffee in the afternoon, dinner followed by occasional trips to the bar in the evening.

However we were making great progress and our solution and recommendations were coming along nicely. We could see what the company needed to do, where it had to change strategy, what its future could be if it implemented our proposals and all in all we were feeling pretty happy with ourselves. Nevertheless I couldn't help looking up or around the room from time to time to see if my mysterious man in black with the red eyes had joined us, but he never did.

Well that is until much later that night when we'd all packed up for the evening, gone to the bar for a nightcap before they closed, decided that we'd done enough for today and that we'd meet early next morning to start working on the actual presentation of our findings and recommendations. We'd done the work. We'd reached our conclusions. Now we had to present it to the other two syndicates and the tutors.

Finally we all bid each other good night and my three companions left the old building to go to their bedrooms in the new block and as I wandered into the hallway to go upstairs to my room I felt really weary. This project was hard, mentally demanding and I like the others had simply had enough for today and so I decided to go straight up to bed.

CHAPTER 5

Why I did it I don't know, but instead of heading up the stairs I found myself walking to Maple room and as I entered there he was sitting at the table where he'd been before.

'I've been expecting you' he said his red eyes dull as he stood and moved to the mantelpiece where with a black candle in each hand he looked at me before turning and placing one at each end of the shelf. I didn't see him use a match or lighter but suddenly the wicks were alight and a dull flame was flickering above each of them as the room took on the distinctive smell of candles burning.

'Look what the hell do you think you're doing?' I asked edging towards the door.

'Hell again? You are obsessed with Hell, aren't you? Why is that I wonder? Have you been there? Are you going there? Do you want to go there? Where is Hell? What is Hell for that matter?'

Another odd thing was that when he moved I didn't see him change from one location to another. One moment he was in one place and the next in a blink of an eye he was in another. So it was now, as he was no longer standing by the mantelpiece but sitting at the table again.

'Sit down we have much to discuss' he demanded quietly.

'We do?'

'Oh yes. You'd be surprised how much we need to talk about'.

I did as he asked thinking that this was crazy. Here was I a grown man talking to some apparition and yet unlike the noises and voices that I'd suffered in the second floor bedroom, I wasn't frightened now, just curious. Suddenly I also no longer felt tired but surprisingly wide awake.

'So what do we need to talk about?' I asked curiously.

'Life. Death. Things in-between. Strange things. Happy things. Sad things. Your fascination with Hell ....'

'I'm not fascinated with Hell' I interrupted angrily.

'Really?' and he raised an eyebrow. Don't you want to know what it's like?'

'No I don't. I've no interest in that at all'.

'Really?'

'Look stop saying really. I know what I'm interested in and what I'm not. In fact I'm not really interested in talking to you any more at all so I'm going'.

'No you're not'.

'Try and stop me!'

'Oh I will but not by physical force. I'll stop you leaving by another type of force'.

'What force?'

'The force of argument. I'll persuade you to stay'.

'Go on then just you try' I snapped as I moved nearer to the door.

'You are Greg Thorbone. You are almost thirty one years old. You are single but have in the past had a number of girlfriends. In fact in many ways you are a feckless sort of chap with women as you don't seem to settle down but hop from one to another including hopping from one bed to another. You've slept with Belinda while you've been here in my home and you want to sleep with her again but she won't let you. You also fancy Zoe and Maggie don't you? In fact you'd quite like to get into bed with one or other of them, or maybe both of them? Hey how about that Greg? Are you man enough to service two lusty women who are older than you? They could be very demanding of your sexual prowess, skill and stamina. Be nice to try though wouldn't it?

Of course it wouldn't be the first time you've slept with a much older woman would it? What was her name the one who'd just had her fiftieth birthday? Oh yes I remember. Shirley. That was her and how old were you then? Twenty five was it? So she was twice your age and a year older than your own mother? Tut tut. What a naughty boy you were!

Ah but back to the present day and what about the lovely Loretta? Now there is an attractive woman. More than attractive, simply gorgeous wouldn't you say? I know that's what I would say about her! Quite stunning.

So now then Greg. You tell me now. How am I doing telling you about yourself? I don't think I've missed much out so far have I? Got you about right?'

'Go on' I said now utterly consumed with curiosity and amazement.

'You are to take up a promotion at your company so that is why you are spending time here in my home to learn how to do better at your work. Am I still doing ok?'

'Ye-es so far so good. But how do you know all this?'

'I know everything there is to know about you my friend. In fact there is absolutely nothing about you that I don't know. I know where you were born, where you were brought up, where you went to school'.

'Go on then tell me those things that you say you know'.

To my amazement he then smiled and leaning back recounted my early life, my upbringing, my schools, my football injury that I sustained when I collided with the goal post and was carted off to hospital an accident which left me with a scar to my forehead which is still with me to this day. He talked about my parents, my uncle and aunt, my grandparents. He described the houses in which we lived, the street where I played, my bicycle which I used to ride to the local park and where I met up with some pals and we played hide and seek, or pretended to be soldiers, or climbed the trees, or played on the swings and roundabout. Eventually I held up both hands palm out towards him.

'Ok ok I give up. So you know everything there is to know about me. But how? How can do you that?'

He smiled. 'Because I can see into your soul and a man's soul tells me everything about him'.

'My soul?'

'Umm. Now your soul is telling me that deep down if you are honest with yourself and therefore that means you will be honest with me, then you *do* want to know about Hell'.

'Do I?'

'Yes you do Greg. Hell is an often maligned institution and I'd like to help change your perception of it'.

'Why?'

'Because that is what I do'.

'Here. Just here?'

'This is my home'.

'Yes you said that before. What do you mean it is your home? It isn't. It is owned by the College'.

'Ah a common misconception. The College like to think they own it and everyone who comes here thinks that too but the real owner is me. I've been here for so many years that is why I say this is my home'.

'So are you the man who built this house or his son that was killed in the fire?'

'No I was here on this site long before that'.

'But my understanding is that there was nothing here before the original man decided to build the house all those years ago?'

'Wrong. Hundreds of years ago I was here under the ground and they built the house on top of me'.

'Oh come on don't be stupid'.

He looked at me and his eyes changed from dull red to bright burning red and they seemed to sear into me so much so that I had to look away. When I looked up he was no longer sitting at the table but standing by the window with one hand holding the curtains, but once again I hadn't seen him physically move.

'Now I've got something to show you' he smiled.

'What?'

'Hell' and with that he eased back the long thick curtain which not only covered the window but also the wall below it. But as the material rolled back it revealed not the window to the outside that I was expecting and which I was sure had been there before, but a black door.

'Come and look' he invited as he turned the handle and pulled the door open towards him. From within, whatever was there emanated a dull glow. It was difficult to describe the colour as it seemed to change. Initially I thought it was purple, then red, then bright orange, then a kind of dull green but as I peered from where I was I could see a staircase leading down which curled to the right and so went out of sight making it impossible to see how long it was or where it led.

'Come closer' he instructed and much against my will I found myself walking towards that door. 'Look down' he suggested and suddenly he seemed to be standing beside me. 'Hell is through that door. Hell is down there. Now just look who is waiting to meet you there?'

As I peered down suddenly Zoe appeared from around the corner coming up the stairs. She was partly obscured from the waist downwards by what seemed to be swirling smoke, but she was stark naked, smiling and beckoning me towards her as she said quietly 'Come on Greg I'm here for you'.

'And so am I' said Maggie as she also unexpectedly appeared beside Zoe. She was also naked and attractive in a somewhat chunky way but what drew my eyes were her truly huge breasts and like the other woman her lower half seemed unclear but slipping her arm around Zoe's waist she pulled her close into her side. 'You could have us both if you like if you're up to it?' she offered, then as the other woman looked at her she leaned forward and popped a little kiss on Zoe's lips.

Both women turned to me and swaying provocatively smiled as Maggie asked 'Would you like that?'

'You know you would like to have us both wouldn't you? That's what you want isn't it? And here we are all ready for you' simpered Zoe in support.

'Both of us' smirked Maggie holding out a hand towards me. 'Come on Greg'. It'll be wonderful'.

I stood and stared at the scene before me. Two early middle aged women stark naked offering themselves to me. Around them seemed to be a sort of haze and their heads and faces were framed from behind with a glow of deep colours which yet again constantly seemed to change from deep purple to dark green to dull red to a kind of burnt orange before fading to purple again as the two women turned and walked away down the stairs, around the corner and so out of my sight.

Immediately they were replaced with a succession of faces of past girlfriends who faded into and then immediately out of vision before they in turn were replaced by the long blonde hair of Loretta the professor who'd lectured us the other day. She was wearing the same outfit again of a short pleated pink skirt and a white blouse.

'Hello Greg have you been looking for me? Well here I am' and slowly and seductively she unbuttoned her blouse and discarded it revealing the most beautiful and perfectly shaped breasts I think I'd ever seen. 'Nice?' she smiled as flicking her tongue across her lips she twisted to look downwards at her hip and then used both hands to run down the side zip.

I gazed enthralled as the skirt slithered down her legs revealing tan coloured stockings, a white suspender belt and pink panties that matched the skirt she'd just taken off. 'I'm all ready for you' she whispered holding out both hands and leaning forward towards me. 'Follow me' she invited turning her back. As the mist cleared I stared at her buttocks wiggling delightfully as her long legs took her down the stairs and out of sight.

'See' said Belinda dressed in a sweater and jeans who now appeared to replace Loretta, 'just because you can't have me again there's no need for you to miss out on your sexual delights is there?'

Then she too was gone as the man with the red eyes took my arm and twisting me to look at him said softly and reassuringly 'Greg you've seen what is waiting for you. And there's more, so much more. Hell isn't bad. In fact some of it is really rather nice and I'll help you find those parts shall I?'

As I looked at him his eyes which had varied between dull and bright red faded to a complete blankness. For a moment there seemed nothing there as he said 'Shall we go together? Let me be your guide?'

'No I don't think so'.

Instantly the blankness in his eyes disappeared and they grew larger and glowed the most terrible penetratingly bright red and deep within them as well as being able to suddenly see flames leaping and flashing extraordinarily I could also hear the sounds of fire crackling and when he spoke again this time his voice was angry, harsh aggressive and demanding.

'No? Whatever do you mean no? Yes is the answer. Yes is the *only* answer. Yes. It is the time Greg. Stop hesitating. Everything is all there waiting for you. No more delay. Come with me. *Come NOW*'.

'NO' I yelled leaping back. 'GET AWAY. I don't want anything more to do with you, or that door, or what is down those stairs or anything that you represent'.

With a cry I turned to run out of the room into the

corridor but it was hard to move as my feet and legs seemed to be enmeshed in something that completely prevented them from moving at all never mind trying to run. I struggled to break free and got increasingly panicky as whatever it was wrapping itself around my legs the more I strove to get free from it the more it entangled me. More and more.

But abruptly and with a supreme effort I wrenched one leg free and soon after the other also became clear and at last I found myself moving. Running. I was free.

Then I woke up drenched in sweat.

Quickly I sat up and switched on the bedside light and saw that my feet were twisted around the sheet which seemed to have come un-tucked from the mattress and was tangled with the duvet around my lower legs.

I wasn't in the syndicate room called Maple but my bedroom on the first floor and I realised I'd had an extremely strange and very frightening dream.

I lay there for a while thinking it though. It must have been a mixture of my memory and my conscience interacting with each other fuelled by perhaps one nightcap too many coupled with the mental strains of the project. Certainly after I'd left the bar and the other three had walked out of the old building to go to their rooms in the new block I had stood at the bottom of the stairs for a moment and wondered about going to see if anything or anyone was in Maple, but whether through fear, disinterest or just plain old tiredness I'd decided not to do that and had climbed wearily to my own room, stripped off, peed, washed, done teeth and got into bed where I'd dropped off straight away and while I slept I'd had this bizarre and awful dream.

Gradually I allowed myself to relax and eventually I dropped off to sleep again and this time I slept soundly right through to morning when the alarm woke me at six.

It didn't take me long to shower, shave and get dressed and I was downstairs in the coffee room where I met up with Maggie and Zoe and moments later Richard also came in. We chatted, kicked a couple of other ideas around then agreed that we'd get an hour's work done before we went into breakfast so we all helped ourselves to another mug of coffee and trooped off to Maple room. I was in the lead and taking a deep breath I pushed open the door and led the way inside. I strode to the curtained window and yanked back the heavy material.

There was a window. No black door. No steps down. No strange light radiating from within. No naked women. No man with red eyes.

Just a plain ordinary window through which I could see the gardens, the immaculately manicured lawns, various trees and shrubs on one of which a little way away sitting on a branch a cheerful little robin was peering in at me.

Giving a gentle sigh of relief I moved away and headed towards the table and we settled down to our work.

CHAPTER 6

Later that morning we presented our findings to the two tutors and the other eight members of the course. We were the second syndicate to speak and when we'd finished we felt that we'd done a better job on the complex project than the first syndicate and so were feeling pretty pleased with ourselves.

Unfortunately however when the third group stood up and presented it was clear that they'd done an even better job on the multifaceted task than we had. They'd come up with some points that we seemed to have missed, and some of the elements of their solution were definitely more innovative and creative then either our syndicate or the first to present had developed.

As Tony and Janet had indicated a discussion by all twelve of us took us through to lunch time and then the afternoon was taken up with a full and thorough class discussion of the whole project, the findings, the learnings that we'd got out of it and the relevance of its key points to our own businesses and real life.

We finished around five and were free until seven thirty when we all met in the bar where Tony bought us all drinks and when we went into dinner sitting on our table were several bottles of red and white wine as Janet announced that drinks tonight at the gala dinner were on the college.

I finally stumbled off to bed around twelve thirty, quite well oiled but not drunk, disappointed that Belinda had turned me down again for a last night bonking session and so I went to bed alone and slept like a log.

Next morning, my last at the college, dawned dull and

wet. After breakfast we congregated in the main lecture room for the last time and spent an interesting morning reviewing the whole four weeks reminding ourselves of the many and varied things that we'd studied and learnt while there.

Finally it was over and after the prizes for best syndicate which disappointingly wasn't ours but the ones who'd gone third in the big presentation; third, second and overall best individual course members had been presented at which I was pleased to receive the third prize but after a moment of disappointment that it wasn't me that won nevertheless a genuine feeling of pleasure as Belinda walked out to receive her first prize.

Lunch surprisingly was quite a sombre affair as we knew that the friendships or acquaintanceships that we'd formed over the past four weeks were now going to end and although we all assured each other that we would *definitely* keep in touch, the reality was that we all knew that we probably wouldn't.

So I shook hands with everyone, hugged Zoe and Maggie, kissed Belinda and went to my room to finish packing which didn't take long as I'd done most of it when I got up earlier that morning. I took my bags to my car and then remembering that I'd not left the room key at reception I walked slowly back into the college main hall, waving at a couple of the others as they went out of the door to their cars.

Having dropped the key in the basket left on the reception desk for that purpose I was about to walk out, but on an impulse decided to have one final look at Maple syndicate room which had featured so vividly in my dream.

Pushing open the door I walked inside. There was nothing obviously untoward but surprisingly the centre room light was switched on because the window curtain was pulled closed.

I walked around the room and I don't know what made me stop and look closely at the mantelpiece but I did and I stared at it in sheer disbelief. Because at each end of the wooden ledge was a small pile of wax.

Black candle wax.

'No' I muttered as I recoiled sharply then turning I couldn't stop myself walking over to the window curtain. Quickly I tugged it back and gazed with incredulity as there was no window. No view to the outside. No robin on a branch.

Just a solid black door.

THE END

Somehow our Devils are never quite what we expect when we meet them face to face.
Nelson DeMille.

Each of us bears our own Hell.
Virgil

> ***Hell is oneself.***
> ***Hell is alone, the other figures in it merely projections.***
> ***T S Eliot.***

CONCLUSION

So there we are. You've come to the end.

However the question I posed at the beginning of this book remains unanswered.

Do ghosts exist?

Maybe? Maybe not?

Will anyone ever really know?

I doubt it.

But until they do then I wouldn't like to say for definite whether I think they do or not. Hopefully though you've enjoyed these four stories. Perhaps they made your hair prickle on the back of your neck? If it has and also made you think then that is exactly what I wanted to do.

Thank you for reading this my sixth book.

MIKE UPTON

**Other titles by Mike Upton
and available from AuthorHouse
are shown on the following pages.**

AMBITIONS END©

Ambitions End was Mike Upton's first novel and is a story of Ambition and one man's quest to avenge his father.

As a teenager Mark Watson sees the devastating effect on his parents when his father's business is bankrupted and he vows to get even with the industrialist who caused this event.

The book follows Mark's early years, schooling, his entry into the business world and his single minded climb up the corporate ranks until he becomes Chief Executive of a multi-national conglomerate.

His marriage, affairs and tangled love life are interwoven throughout the fast moving story which alternates between Britain, America and Europe as Mark manages his increasingly complex business empire whilst never losing sight of his long term goal.

He ruthlessly exploits and discards people, manoeuvres, manipulates and plots using all means at his disposal. Industrial espionage, blackmail all find a place in his pitiless progress as he seeks to achieve his overriding ambition to gain revenge for his father.

As the story reaches a climax one question is on

the readers mind and that question is – will Mark Watson reach the end of his Ambition?

Ambitions End draws on Mike's own business experience honed over many years to create a story with authenticity, interest and excitement.

WINNERS NEVER LOSE©

Winners Never Lose, Mike's second novel is the sequel to Ambitions End.

This time it starts in the Oil Industry as primary character Mark Watson once again generates his own unique, tough and demanding approach to this complex industry before he is head hunted into the Pharmaceutical Industry where he hones and develops his skills to turn an ailing business around to regain its former good financial results.

He has to find out who is leaking vital information to competitors and stop it, whilst at the same time re-energising the company's complex but moribund new product development programmes; manage and defeat cut throat competition; sell off unprofitable companies within the Group and acquire competitors. His wheeling and dealing is much to the fore as he tackles the challenges in these two important industries.

As well as seeing and understanding Mark's tough minded approach to the business problems, difficulties and opportunities that emerge during the story we also see how he copes with the tragedy of the loss of a child and follow his continued betrayal of his wife with a string of affairs.

The juxtaposition of Mark's ruthless attitude to business and people interwoven into his complex personal life creates a fast moving, interesting and absorbing story where the action moves from Britain to America, India and Europe before finally finishing in Australia.

Winners Never Lose, like his first novel Ambitions End, draws on Mike's extensive knowledge and experience of large multi-national corporations. His first hand familiarity with the way that big business operates is fully utilised in this exciting and fast paced novel.

ARROW OF TRUTH©

Arrow of Truth is Mike's third novel and his first "who-dun-it".

The story tells how William Hardy the third generation owner and Chairman of a family manufacturing business, struggles to keep his business going in the face of increased demands from his customers and ruthless competition from his competitors as well as suffering arson attacks, bomb threats and blackmail letters from an unknown assailant. But he is finding business life more and more difficult and doesn't have the natural business flair of his forebears.

Meanwhile the company's bank believing that the business is on the verge of bankruptcy installs a team of specialist turnaround experts to work with him to try and save the business from collapse and then rebuild it towards its former glories and fortunes. Tensions rise and challenges appear as the turnaround team take over from William leaving him feeling frustrated and sidelined.

But while William is battling with these complex and demanding business issues, he is totally unaware that his wife, obsessed with a secret lover is betraying and cheating on him. However in a twist of delightful irony it is also she who is betrayed by her lover but not in the way that might be expected.

Set in Norfolk in the East of England, the story is a fast moving thriller set within a business background where the many characters and events interact with each other, as they unfold towards the surprising ending.

Arrow of Truth (like his previous novels - Ambitions End and Winners Never Lose) draws on Mike's considerable experience and knowledge of business in general and turnaround teams in particular and how they operate to try and save businesses that are in difficulty.

THE BOSS©

The Boss is Mike's fourth novel and is a challenging story set in the world of business and tells how Helen Buckley, an accountant by training and profession, attempts to fight her way to the top in a highly competitive and difficult corporate world controlled and dominated by men.

It follows her early life, her many love affairs, her marriage and the reasons for its failure, as well as charting her progress as she struggles to prove that she is as good as a man in solving company problems and confronting business difficulties.

Innovative in finding solutions to business problems, she gains a reputation as an expert wheeler dealer which leads her to decide to branch out on her own by setting up her own business consultancy which soon becomes highly successful.

However the stress of her business life leads her on an increasingly steep downward path towards alcoholism which threatens to destroy her business, her personal relationships and ultimately, her life.

Her battle against the ravages and effects of alcoholism are well and accurately documented as are her attempts to overcome the effects of this awful illness.

The Boss is a moving and sensitive story, with

an interesting twist in that there is choice of two different endings.

A TWIST IN THE TALE©

A Twist in the Tale - my fifth book - is a collection of four different stories of varying lengths and subjects, but all of them have a surprise at the end. An unexpected twist - hence the title.

Two of them were originally conceived as plots to be turned into full length books but as I had always wanted to write a book of short stories then the decision was taken to use these ideas and thoughts as they stood and turn each into a short story in its own right. The topics are widely varied but hopefully that adds to the interest of the book.

Sea Deep. Advertising man Pete loses his high flying job in London and so after struggling to find something similar or better, to the dismay of his wife he decides to pursue a dream and embark on a wholly new way of life?

Illusion. During the Second World War a chance meeting between an 11 year old boy exploring the moors above his village and an Italian prisoner of war in a newly constructed prison camp leads the lad in later life to pursue a dream. But dreams don't always have happy endings.

Choice. Dave is head of marketing for a company making a range of cleaning products. While trying to decide on which of three potential advertising agencies to choose also has to make a choice about his personal and private life but having made that decision fate intervenes in an unexpected and threatening way.

Gone. One Sunday afternoon in winter, a happily married and successful middle aged businessman walks out of his house to find out why his dogs seem restless, but he doesn't come back. He simply disappears. Why? Where has he gone and who is the mysterious Bulgarian lady? A tense thriller unfolds as the police uncover information about his secret double life.

TO LEARN MORE ABOUT MIKE UPTON
VISIT HIS WEBSITE

www.mikeuptonauthor.com

========================